Midge _____ _____ Garcia in _____ California Health Spa?

That's one of the questions you have to answer to win $15,000.

But you'll have some help in your search in the person of Matthew Prize, ace detective, professor of criminology and chocolate addict. As his health-conscious girl friend Jan hides his Milky Ways and Baby Ruths, you can follow him as he tracks down clues and uncovers the secrets of the suntanned, wealthy suspects, all of whom seem so very innocent.

The scene of the crime is a fancy aerobics salon for women. The possible culprits are the rich and mighty denizens of one of California's most glamorous beach communities.

But the crime is strictly murder!

A $ WHODUNIT ? $ MYSTERY #1

PRIZE MEETS MURDER

R.T. EDWARDS WITH OTTO PENZLER

PUBLISHED BY POCKET BOOKS NEW YORK

Another *Original* publication of POCKET BOOKS

POCKET BOOKS, a division of Simon & Schuster, Inc.
1230 Avenue of the Americas, New York, N.Y. 10020

Copyright © 1984 by Whodunit, Inc.

ISBN: 0-671-50988-8

First Pocket Books printing June, 1984

10 9 8 7 6 5 4 3 2 1

POCKET and colophon are registered trademarks
of Simon & Schuster, Inc.

Printed in the U.S.A.

$15,000 REWARD

If You Can Solve The Mystery In
PRIZE MEETS MURDER
$Whodunit?$ #1

CONTEST RULES

I. How to Enter. Complete Official Entry Form on the next page. Then attach it to any 8½" × 11" paper on which you have printed or typed your answers to the following four questions:

1. What is the name of the person who killed Midge Branner and Ernie Garcia?
2. What was the motive for the crimes?
3. What four clues enabled Matthew Prize to eliminate all but one of the possible suspects?
4. Which of the four clues above involved the kidnapping of Jan Early?

Clearly print your name, address and telephone number on each sheet and answer <u>all</u> questions completely. Then mail entry to: CRIMESOLVER'S CONTEST, P.O. Box 1094, Ridgely, MD 21683. Enter as many different solutions as you wish, but each entry must be mailed separately and must be accompanied by an Official Entry Form plus a 50¢ processing fee (check or money order only, payable to CRIMESOLVER'S CONTEST). All entries must be received by August 15, 1984 and will not be returned. Official Entry Forms may not be copied or mechanically reproduced. All entries must be in English.

II. Judging. Correct answers for each question have been determined by the authors and are in a sealed bank vault. All entries will be reviewed under the supervision of Beaumont-Bennett, Inc., an independent judging organization, whose decisions will be final. If more than one entry (or no entry) has the correct answers to <u>all four</u> questions, contest winner will be the entrant who, in the opinion of the authors, has best expressed the correct answers to <u>question number 3</u>, as Matthew Prize <u>himself</u> would have expressed it, using the fewest possible words. The best answer to <u>question 3</u> will be the one that is closest in meaning, logic and style of expression to the actual words the authors have used, which will be found in the vault. In the case of a tiebreaker, the authors' decision will be final.

Clue: To improve your chances of winning, answer <u>question 3</u> as if you were Matthew Prize answering it in the book—and don't waste any words!

III. Reward. Contest winner will be notified by mail on or before October 7, 1984 and, upon verification, will be awarded $15,000 by no later than November 30, 1984. No transfer or substitution of prize permitted. Taxes on prize are winner's responsibility.

IV. Winning Solutions. Contest winner and winning solution will be announced at the Mysterious Book Shop 129 West 56th Street, New York, New York 10019 on or before October 15, 1984. For name of winner, send a stamped, self-addressed envelope to: WINNER, P.O. Box 669-D, Ridgely, MD 21660. Requests received after November 30, 1984 will not be fulfilled. For a copy of authors' answers to the contest questions, send a separate stamped, self-addressed envelope, plus 25¢ for handling, to: PRIZE SOLUTION, P.O. Box 669-D1, Ridgely, MD 21660. Requests for solution will be fulfilled after October 7, 1984 but not later than November 30, 1984.

V. Eligibility. Contest open only to residents of continental U.S. and Canada (excluding residents of Quebec), age 18 or older, except the authors and their families, and employees and their immediate families, of Simon & Schuster, its subsidiaries, advertising agencies and Beaumont-Bennett, Inc. Contest is void in Florida, Vermont and wherever prohibited or restricted by law and is subject to all federal, state and local regulations. Winner will be required to sign an affidavit of eligibility and a release form permitting use of winner's name and likeness for publicity purposes.

Please note: Requests without applicable fees or postage will not be honored or returned. No responsibility will be assumed for any late or misdirected mail in connection with this contest. No correspondence about this contest will be entered into, acknowledged or returned.

PRIZE MEETS MURDER
$WHODUNIT?$ #1 Contest

Please print or type all information requested on this form and attach it to one or more 8½″ × 11″ sheets on which you have answered the 4 questions indicated below. All entries must be in English.

Name_____

Address_____

City_____ State_____ Zip_____

Telephone (___)_____

Question 1. What is the name of the person who killed Midge Branner and Ernie Garcia?

Question 2. What was the motive for the crimes?

Question 3. What four clues enabled Matthew Prize to eliminate all but one of the possible suspects?

Important Note: If more than one entry, or no entry, has the correct answers to all four questions, the contest winner will be the entrant who, in the opinion of the authors, has best expressed the correct answers to this question (question 3) as Matthew Prize himself would have expressed it, using the fewest possible words. The best answer to this question will be the one that is closest in meaning, logic and style of expression to the actual words the authors have used, which will be found in the vault.

Cut Carefully Along This Line

Clue: To improve your chances of winning, answer this question as if you were Matthew Prize answering it in the book.

Question 4. Which of the four clues above involved the kidnapping of Jan Early?

Mail this completed form, plus 50¢ processing fee by check or money order   payable to:

CRIMESOLVER'S CONTEST
P.O. BOX 1094
RIDGELY, MD 21683

NOTE: This Official Entry Form must be used and may not be copied or reproduced. See official Contest Rules for complete details. **Entries must be received by August 15, 1984.**

PRIZE
MEETS
MURDER

Chapter 1

—————————————

THURSDAY STARTED EARLY. AT LEAST A good hour too early, on a misty gray October morning.

Matthew Prize sat up suddenly in bed. Something had fallen over in his study down the hall, something that hit the floor with a clattering bang. After glancing at the clock and determining it was only 7:15 A.M., Matt swung out of the wide bed.

He was a long, lean man of thirty-three, sandy-haired and, at the moment, wearing the trousers of a pair of candy-striped pajamas.

There were noises coming from his study now. Shuffling, banging, muttering. Outside his beach cottage the Pacific Ocean was making its usual surf-across-the-sand sounds.

He moved barefooted along the chill hall floor, halted on the threshold of his small office. "Hush," he suggested.

A slim blond young woman, clad in dark blue running shorts and a lighter blue jersey, was crouched on the rug gathering up the spilled contents of his In-Out box. "Morning, sluggard," she said, without looking up.

"Jan," Matt said, "I love you with a passion that knows no bounds. You are a thing of beauty and a joy forever. But why the hell are you banging around in here at the crack of dawn?"

"Oh, dawn cracked a good hour ago," Jan Early replied, rising to face him. She was a pretty young woman, with a trace of freckles on her tan face. Next month she'd be twenty-seven. "Anyway, I had an idea for a new article so I—"

"Why aren't you out running along the beach?" He avoided the spill of papers on the floor and walked to the crowded bookshelves that climbed high up one wall.

"I did that already." Jan settled into his desk chair and smiled at him. "You really ought to start exercising yourself, Matt. You're getting a bit seedy."

Perched in front of a row of law books was a squat jar of bright-colored M&Ms. "I'm in excellent shape," he assured her as he snatched a handful of candy.

"Ugh!" She turned away. "A chocolate addict, a junk-food junkie." She sighed.

"I'm only doing this for the sake of research, so I can write *Confessions of a Southern California Chocolate Eater*." He started popping candy into his mouth. "Surefire best-seller."

"It's not funny really," she said. "Here I am writing for *Vegetarian News* and *Healthy Runner* magazines while you . . . you're a nutritional basket case."

"I know, I know." He took another handful. "I just

thank my lucky stars I'm so charming that you put up with me despite all my moral flaws."

"Yes, that shows a definite weakness in my character," the young woman said. "With you it's chocolate, with me it's Matt Prize, Associate Professor of Criminology at Cal State, San Amaro Campus."

He sat in the room's only other chair, a disreputable old leather armchair. "What're you writing?"

"Tell you when I've finished."

"What time did you arise?"

"Six."

"I didn't even notice."

"You were sleeping off last night's junk food binge."

"Pizza isn't junk food." He stood up. "I read in some prestigious sheet, either the Los Angeles *Times* or the *National Enquirer,* that pizza is the perfect food. Provides you with protein, carbo—"

"Hooey," she said.

"That, too." He crossed, rested his hand on her shoulder. "You realize, don't you, that my first class at CS today isn't until eleven?"

"I didn't mean to knock that thing over and wake you," Jan said. "But the clutter on your desk makes it next to impossible not to—"

"What you see is not exactly clutter." He nodded at the piles of test papers, file folders, letters, newspaper and magazine clippings, and other assorted paper ephemera. "It's simply that I have an unorthodox system of filing."

"So do pack rats."

"Pack rats have survived for countless centuries, and they have very little in the way of stress-related diseases." He kissed the back of her neck. "Want to have lunch at some posh seaside bistro today?"

"Can't. I want to finish this piece and then I'm starting that new class this afternoon."

He frowned. "Class?"

"Not at your dippy college, Matt. Down at the Diana Aerobic Salon."

"I remember now." He grinned. "But don't you get enough exercise from—"

"This is something I want to try," she said. "Plus which I think I can sell an article on aerobic dancing to one of my editors."

"Diana Salon," he said, wandering to the window. "Didn't that used to be Reinman's Gym?" The morning was gray, the stretch of sandy beach between his cottage and the ocean was blurred by mist. Twists of fog were drifting in over the water, along with a few early-rising sea gulls.

"It was, yes. But they renovated the gym at the same time the new marina and yacht harbor was built in the heart of seaside San Amaro. It's very chic now, doesn't smell of perspiration at all."

"Max Reinman still runs the place, doesn't he?" A somewhat forlorn gull was prowling across Matt's mixture of scraggly lawn and beachfront, hunting for something illusive.

"He does. Matter of fact, Reinman is interested in my writing some sort of brochure to plug his new salon. Another reason I am taking the aerobic dancing class."

"Crass and mercenary."

"Caught it from you," Jan said. "After all, you were a licensed private investigator here in the Los Angeles area for almost six years and there's nobody crasser than a private eye."

"Only in books and on television," he said, leaving

the window. "In real life college profs are much more money hungry."

"Which is why you fit in so well at Cal State."

"Our third year in business at that location." He returned to the armchair. "Would it annoy you if I fried up some pork sausage for breakfast?"

"Yes, but don't let that deter you."

"Now I know what Romeo and all those other star-crossed lovers felt like," he said. "Ah, to be hopelessly in love with a health food nut when one is a junk food freak. Sad and tragic."

"What you're doing to your insides is tragic," she said. "But I'll try to concentrate on your handsome exterior."

"My best side."

Hunching her slender shoulders, she swung around to face the manual typewriter that sat on his desk amid the clutter. "I love you," she said. "Now go take a shower or something so I can type up a few notes to myself for this new article."

Matt walked over to her. Gently and carefully he lifted her from the chair and placed her facing him. Putting his arms around her, he kissed her. "I get lonesome showering alone," he said after a moment.

Curt Sloane said, "Forty-nine . . . fifty." With a satisfied nod, he got up off the living-room floor. He was a slender man of thirty-seven, blond, not more than five feet six. "You're going to love it."

His wife Connie was two years younger than he and about fifteen pounds overweight. She was sitting in the kitchen, stirring a spoonful of sugar substitute into her morning coffee. "But I'm clumsy," she said.

Curt came into the yellow-and-white kitchen. "Would I live with a clumsy lady?"

Connie smiled faintly, shrugged. "I'll go through with it," she promised. "But I don't see why I couldn't just exercise at home the way you do. You're in marvelous shape and you just do push-ups and sit-ups and—"

"We've tried that, Con, and you don't stick with it." He poured himself a cup of coffee and then joined her at the round café table. "This way, though, you'll be going to the salon three times a week. You'll do your aerobic dancing and in no time—trust me, love—you'll be fit and happy . . . in no time."

"I'm as happy as I want to be already." She ran her right hand through her tousled dark hair.

"But besides getting yourself into shape, you'll meet new people."

"New people who might turn into customers for you."

Curt's eyes narrowed. "Hey, Con, I don't work that way. I'm not pushing you into something just so I can find more people who want to buy and sell houses," he said evenly. "I really think this'll be fun for you."

"Anyway, I know too many people already. I'm forever having to rescue Susan when her darn VW breaks down, and then I get roped into watching Nancy's three imps when she goes off to—"

"Mrs. Mott told me she loved the class she took at the Diana Aerobic Salon."

"Mrs. Mott." Her nose wrinkled.

"Okay, she's a phony bitch," he admitted. "But she is on the brink of buying that Berrill house over on LaPaloma Drive. The commission on that'll be very nice."

"It'll mean we can finally pay off Dr. Holland and the San Amaro Bank and Trust and—"

"Look, we've been in a slump the past year or so." He sipped his coffee. "The real estate business was hurt by the economic decline. But now, Con, things are—"

"Seems like we've been in a slump for the past ten years. Boom times or bad."

He set his cup down. "You know I'm a damned good salesman." He looked straight at her. "And you know sure as hell that Dick Meskin wouldn't keep me on at Seamark Realty if I was a loser."

"Yes, I do know, Curt. I'm sorry," said his wife. "Didn't mean to nag . . . I'll let you know tonight how the first class went."

"Relax, Con, you're going to love it," he assured her.

She let the phone ring.

It rang eleven times and died.

Midge Branner hugged herself, getting a sudden attack of gooseflesh. She was sitting at the small table in the tiny kitchen of her second-floor apartment. Down on Mar Vista Drive an early morning bus went rumbling by.

"Don't forget," she reminded herself, "this place is conveniently located."

"Sure, on the wrong side of the tracks."

"True, but only six blocks from the salon."

Midge, an attractive dark-haired woman of thirty-one, had been teaching aerobic dancing classes at Max Reinman's for five months, since two weeks after the refurbished gym had opened up.

17

"Not exactly dancing on Broadway, is it?"

She got up from the table, carried her juice glass and cereal bowl over to the sink. There was a green coppery stain at the sink bottom that absolutely nothing could remove.

No matter. Street noise, stained sink, ancient plumbing. It was still better than life before. And when you looked out the small, high kitchen window, and stretched a bit, you got a lovely view of beach and palm trees.

The phone started ringing again.

Kept ringing.

"Leave me alone," she said. "Please."

Ten rings this time before it stopped.

She wasn't going back. Even if it meant she'd be teaching classes at Max's salon until she was old and gray.

"Today's afternoon class, though," she said as she washed her breakfast dishes, "that'll be something special to get through."

Well, maybe not. Maybe there wouldn't be any trouble. But ever since she'd seen the list with the names of the nine women who'd signed up for the new four o'clock session that started today, she'd been uneasy.

"I just wish they'd leave me alone."

She was strong enough to hold out. She'd come this far.

She nodded to herself.

"They aren't going to beat me."

The phone began to ring again.

Lizbeth Wagner glanced at herself in the hall mirror before she entered the dining room.

"Scary, isn't it, Sis?"

"Do you know what's comforting about you, Kevin?" she said to the dark, thirty-year-old man at the head of the table. "You're so very dependable. You were a nasty little toad as a boy and you've never changed."

"You've changed," said Kevin Wagner. "Lots of new wrinkles on that famous face that once launched a thousand ad campaigns." He picked up his coffee cup with his left hand. "And there's a slight sag in your—"

"Thirty-four isn't over the hill, dear."

"Models are like boxers, Sis. Washed up at thirty." He made a slurping noise as he drank his coffee.

"Kevin, must you—"

He laughed. "Whoa now. Don't go criticizing your host," he advised. "You're living off my bounty, so you—"

"Father's bounty. He founded Wagner Electronics and you only inherited it," she said. "You've been lucky so far not to run the whole damned company into the ground."

Kevin held up his hand in a stop-it gesture. "Aw, let's not squabble, Sis," he said. "Listen, really, I'm more than happy to have you as my houseguest. House's been sort of empty since my divorce and this reminds me, truly it does, of the good times you and I had as kids."

"I bet." She poured herself some coffee, hand shaking just a bit.

"And I'm also pleased to be funding your course at the Diana Salon," he said. "You're still a handsome woman, and if you can dance around and jiggle some of that extra weight off you and get some of those wrinkles to vanish from your—"

"Once a toad, always a toad. You never . . ." Lizbeth paused when Mrs. Malley walked in from the kitchen to set a silver dish containing a slice of melon at her place.

"You're looking lovely this morning, Miss Lizbeth."

"Why, thank you, Kate."

After the heavyset housekeeper was gone, Kevin shook his head. "Old girl's eyes must be failing."

"Kevin, I've had a rough time the past couple years," said his sister. "My divorce from Brian upset me a good deal and, well, it affected my career, too. Now, though, I feel like trying to—"

"Wasn't the divorce, Sis, it was booze and pills," he cut in, pointing at her with his fork. "Don't forget it. I helped you kick that stuff, too. But I'm not asking for thanks, since I just did my brotherly duty."

Lizbeth dipped her spoon into the pale green of the melon. "I am going to eat this thing," she said, smiling thinly at him. "You are not going to provoke me into leaving the table or into tossing the whole thing into your pasty face, dear."

Chuckling, Kevin spread his hands wide. "Me? Annoy you?" he said, eyebrows going up. "I really do have only your best interests at heart. After all, didn't I suggest this aerobic dancing business in the first place? Knowing full well it's something that'll help you on the road back to—"

"You did suggest it, didn't you?" A frown touched her forehead. "I'm wondering why."

"Because I'm fond of you," he said.

Chapter 2

BY MIDDAY A LIGHT DRIZZLE WAS COMING down on the beach town. Max Reinman stood at the window of his office, gazing across at the San Amaro Marina. Its modern glass, metal, and redwood restaurants and shops managed to glisten in the mist. The sprawling yacht club, all white stone and red tile rooftops, looked as fresh and new as it had the day it opened six months ago. Moored along the docks were yachts, sailboats, ketches and whatever the hell else you called fancy, expensive boats like that. The gently bobbing craft seemed to glow with a special sheen, one that implied big money and the good, easy life.

Max, a squat thickset man in his fifties, felt somewhat like a poor kid with his nose pressed to a bakery shop window. He had a new salon at the edge of the fanciest, most respectable business section of town;

yet he still felt he wasn't quite part of it. The rows of palm trees along the roadway, transplanted from elsewhere, looked sad and downcast to him.

"Just like me," Reinman muttered.

"Beg pardon?"

"Huh?" Reinman returned to his trim, metal desk.

"Sorry, I thought you said something."

"Maybe I did, just talking out loud." He sat, sighing, behind his desk.

"Cheer up, Maxie, don't let this dreadful gloomy weather get you down," advised the tall, handsome young man in the guest chair. He was tanned, broad shouldered, and wore a snug maroon jump suit. His curly hair was a golden blond shade and he smelled faintly of pine cones and old leather. "I know I always get the blues whenever it's so awfully—"

"Look at me, take a good look, Rod," suggested the owner and operator of the Diana Aerobic Salon. "Do I look like a Maxie? No. So don't call me that. Max. That's my name. Max."

Grinning, Rod Flanders crossed his legs. "That's just a dreadful throwback to the days when this place was crowded with sweaty jocks," he told his boss. "All those macho types with low foreheads and brains the size of an anemic peanut."

Reinman said, "Sometimes, my boy, I wish I was back there. Bozos and all. This fancy crap, aerobic dancing and exercise programs . . ." He shrugged. "All these dames from the best parts of town make me nervous."

"But that's where the money is today, Maxie."

"Yeah, sure, I know," he grunted, drumming his stubby fingers on his desk top. "Hell, they closed

down the muni arena three years ago and there ain't
been a bout in this town since. And that fancy new
auditorium next to the Marina, they don't use it for
fights. No, now we got the ballet and the symphony
and this damn—what is it?—schmuck rock."

"Punk rock," corrected Rod.

"Punk, schmuck. A bunch of boys that look like
girls and girls that look like truck drivers. Cut their
hair with a lawn mower, dye it green. Stick pins
through their noses."

"Well, that's show business."

"We don't have enough real hoodlums drifting into
this part of town from the other side of the tracks.
Now they got to import auditoriums full of 'em,"
lamented Reinman. "Kids who'll mug a nun just to
take her rosary beads, kick a blind man, step on a
cripple. I keep telling the cops we need to beef up the
patrols around here nights. I've had a dozen ladies,
very classy dames, complain they're afraid to come
around, even now, at night."

"Oh, it's much better than it was, Maxie."

"Don't seem that way to me, my boy."

Rod uncrossed his legs. "I hesitate to mention this,
since you're in one of your paranoid moods, but—"

"You'd be paranoid, too, whatever that is, if you
had the cash-flow problems I got," Reinman told him.
"With boxers and weight lifters I could get somebody
to lean on them if they didn't pay up. With classy
dames you can't get rough. I mean, I got a rich bitch
from Santa Monica, she owes me eleven hundred
bucks. Yeah, eleven hundred. Says her husband took
the checkbook with him when he went to Stockholm.
He's fooling around in Stockholm with a bunch of

Swedish erotica and I'm on my knees to the gas and electric company so they don't turn off the juice here."

"C'mon, Maxie, don't fib," laughed Rod. "Remember, I help you on the books. We've been showing a healthy profit."

"That's your idea of healthy, I'd hate to see your sick, my boy." He scowled, scratched at his thinning dark hair. "You was mentioning something you didn't want I should know. What?"

"Oh, it's probably nothing," said the handsome dance instructor. "But when I left last evening, quite a bit later than usual, I was almost certain I noticed someone lurking across the street. In that little lane next to the yacht club. Someone keeping an eye on our salon."

Reinman straightened up in his chair. "Who?"

"I wasn't able, unfortunately, to get a good look."

"A big guy maybe, a heavyweight build?"

Shrugging his left shoulder, Rod replied, "Not at all sure, Maxie. It was, you know, merely a fleeting impression. The idea flashed through my mind that this person might be casing our place. But since I had a terribly important engagement elsewhere, and there was no one else left inside, I let the matter pass."

"I been expecting maybe . . ."

"Expecting what?"

Reinman shook his head. "Nothing. Nothing, my boy, outside the usual grief and trouble that's my lot in life," he said. "I should've gone into business with my brother, Abe, back in Florida. Now he owns eight motels, each one a gold mine."

"Why didn't you?"

"We hate each other is why," answered Reinman.

"Now let's talk about this brochure I got this girl Jan Early maybe going to write up for us. You think a nice color shot of you and some of the classier broads'll make a good cover?"

"Obviously," said Rod.

Norm Levine gave an unhappy moan. "This particular watering place may prove too much for my poor old ticker." He was gazing out the wide-view window of Señor Gordito's Mexican Restaurant, watching two slim blondes in white shorts walking away from the row of beachside tennis courts. "All these nubile maidens without and within are—"

"Hasn't married life helped you?" Matt Prize and his curly-haired friend were seated in a booth. It was a few minutes past one in the afternoon.

"Am I married again?" Levine blinked.

"For nearly a year this time."

"Which wife is this?"

"Third."

"Ah, yes. I remember now. Remind me to alert the Guinness chaps and tell them I'm aiming for the Most Wives before the Age of Thirty-Seven Award." He glanced around the crowded restaurant. "That's a very attractive redhead yonder, the lass dipping her mitt in the guacamole."

"Seems to me I heard there's a cure for horniness now." Matt sipped his beer.

"Not my kind. I'm born again horny," explained Levine, staring again out the window. "Can a Jewish lad from a humble home in the Bronx find happiness amidst the glitter of the West? All this flesh and affluence is tempting me sorely. I may sell out to nearby Hollywood or— Wow, what a stunning lady just drove by in that Mercedes. And there's a stunner in a Porsche, another in . . . good gravy, a Rolls no less. Hey, how'd that guy in the old Chevvy get onto Ocean Drive?"

"Let's change the subject and give your system a chance to—"

"Okay. How's Jan?"

"Fine, as usual."

Resting both elbows on the checkerboard tablecloth, Levine asked, "Living together, the way you folks do, does it work?"

"Has so far."

He nodded. "That might be a lot simpler than my method. I keep marrying them," he said. "I don't know, I reckon there's a sentimental streak in me a yard wide. I just adore that marriage ceremony. You know, trotting into the town hall, paying the fee, dragging in two derelicts for witnesses. Gosh, brings tears to my eyes just thinking about it."

"How are things on the paper?"

"No shoptalk. I came here simply to bask in the warmth of your friendship and ogle ladies," said Levine, leaning back. "Dull would be the answer, though, if I were answering. San Amaro, old sock, is a dull town. Outside of a few knifings, gang fights and the like down in the sleazier part of town, and the usual muggings and burglaries hither and yon, it's all quiet on the news front. I'm seriously contemplating asking the San Amaro News-Hour to transfer me to the lovelorn department."

"Maybe you ought to try aerobic dancing."

Levine looked up, left eye narrowing. "What made you mention that?"

"Nothing very sinister, Norm," answered Matt. "Jan's starting an aerobic dancing class this afternoon. I've got the subject on my mind."

"Where?"

"Place with the catchy name of the Diana Aerobic Salon, used to be—"

"Reinman's Gym. I know," said his friend. "I was just rummaging through our files on the joint."

"Why? Something wrong with the place?"

"Not a thing. As good a location as any for bored, wealthy ladies to frolic like gazelles whilst getting in shape."

"But?"

"Remember a boxer named Ernie Garcia?"

"Heavyweight. About five, six years ago he looked like a contender. Then he slipped and dropped out of sight."

"The lad took to doing most of his serious training in saloons and bordellos. That's worse than chocolate and junk food for a jock," said the curly-haired reporter. "He also got into some trouble with the law."

"I remember, yeah. Back three years ago or so." Matt tapped the side of his glass with the tip of his finger. "Something to do with a gang that was looting shipments out at the municipal airport."

"Right. Ernie wasn't the kingpin in the operation, just a minion. Drove cars apparently, did a little strong-arm stuff," he said. "As fate would have it, however, Ernie was the one who got nabbed. Did two and a half years and just got out last week."

"He's in town again?"

"So my reliable sources tell me."

Matt asked, "What's he got to do with the salon?"

"When the joint was a gymnasium, Ernie worked out there pretty regularly. And on the fateful night the cops netted him, he was just a block from the gym."

"Why are you interested in the guy?"

"Human interest story."

"And what else, Norm?"

"Well, there were rumors at the time that Ernie might've had a valuable portion of the loot from the gang's most recent caper with him."

"Police didn't find it?"

"Not a drop, not a speck."

"And Garcia didn't talk about it?"

"Exactly. He was like unto a sphinx when it came to telling whom he was working with or what he might've been in possession of."

"What happened to the gang?"

Levine made a sweeping-away gesture with his left hand. "Vanished in the wind, never pulled another job," he replied. "Imagine they got the wind up and turned their nefarious attentions elsewhere once Ernie was arrested."

Matt drank some more of his beer. "Old news," he decided. "Doesn't have anything to do with Jan and her class."

" 'Course not," agreed Levine.

Chapter 3

MIDGE BRANNER, HANDS ON HIPS, STOOD facing her new class. Eight out of the nine women had shown up, including the one she'd been hoping wouldn't. Midge tried not to notice her.

The rain had grown heavier, was hitting down hard on the slanting skylight of the dance studio. There was also a smudged sea gull perched up on one of the squares of glass.

"First off," Midge was saying, her voice pretty well under control, "for those of you who've never been here to the Diana Salon before, let me answer some important questions. Like where are the rest rooms."

That got the small laugh it usually did from the two rows of women, clad in warm-up suits, sweat pants and shirts, leotards, and shorts and T-shirts, who stood facing her.

Pointing to her left, Midge said, "That door over

yonder leads into Max Reinman's office. Nothing of interest there, just Max and stale cigar smoke. Over on the other side of the room is another door. That connects with a corridor. Red door at the end of the corridor takes you, as some of you've probably already discovered on your own, into the locker-room area. Showers are right next to the locker room. Green door off the corridor is the powder room. The other doors lead to storerooms mostly."

She paused, glancing up at the gray wet afternoon that showed through the high window.

"Let's start off our first get-together with a definition or two," she continued. "A good question to ask up front is, 'What the heck is aerobics anyway?' Well, aerobic exercises are the ones that stimulate your cardiovascular system. Yep, you've all got one." She tapped herself between her breasts. "The system includes your lungs, the muscles of your respiratory system and the most important muscle of all, your heart. Okay, so far? What you'll want to know next is how . . ."

The first session went well, all things considered, and Midge introduced several of the simple slim-dancing exercises that she, after reading several books on the subject and consulting with Rod Flanders, had worked out for her beginning classes. At five minutes after five, when the class ended, most of the women were smiling and perspiring. All but the heaviest woman in the bunch, a plump blond matron who ended up red-faced and wheezing. Midge had a hunch that one wouldn't be coming back.

"That's all until next time, troops," she announced.

"Oh, and if anybody wants her money back, you've got to speak up today or forever hold your peace."

Laughing, smiling, they scattered. Most headed for the corridor that led to the lockers and showers. Jan Early, though, crossed over to knock on Max Reinman's door. And Lizbeth Wagner, hesitantly, came up to Midge.

"I didn't know you were teaching here," she said.

"Oh, so?" Midge bent from the waist, picked up a white towel from the floor, and draped it around her neck.

"Honestly, Midge." She hesitated, then touched the younger woman's arm. "I'd like to stay in the class. I enjoyed it today. Yet if it bothers you to have me here I'll—"

"Nothing bothers me anymore. Not a damn thing. I've developed a strong stomach."

"Listen, Midge, dear, you know I've always—"

"He suggested you come here, didn't he?"

Lizbeth said, "Yes, but he never told me that you were one of the—"

"No, he probably wouldn't," she said. "Okay, stay or go. Up to you, Lizzie. When you see Kevin, tell him to leave me alone."

"What do you mean?"

Midge took a step back from her. "Maybe you don't know about that either," she said. "But if he doesn't stop harassing me . . ." She shook her head, pivoted and went, walking away toward the door that led to the stairway down to the street.

Max Reinman frowned at the cigar in his hand. "Does it bother you if I smoke?"

31

"Yes," answered Jan.

"This don't smell so good to me even." He ground the thing out in a bronze ashtray. "Also it don't help my new image. Right?"

Jan, still wearing her blue warm-up suit, was sitting across from the salon owner. "Frankly, Mr. Reinman, no," she told him. "After all, the Diana Aerobic Salon is dedicated to health and fitness. Cigar smoking really doesn't go with that."

"Yeah, Rod tells me similar stuff." He scowled at the cigar butt. "You can call me Max, by the way."

"I'd rather call you Mr. Reinman," she said. "Tell you why. If I call you Max, that sounds like we're friends. When the time comes for me to ask for money, it's hard to get tough with a friend."

"Hey, listen, Max Reinman never stiffed anybody," he assured her. "You do this writing job, I give you a check." He picked up the pen he used for writing checks.

"Sounds fine."

"Okay, so how much do you want for doing this dinky little brochure?"

"A thousand dollars."

He stiffened in his chair, staring at the slim blonde. "A thousand bucks? I'm not hiring you to write *Gone with the Wind*."

"No, for that I'd charge you a heck of a lot more."

"Five hundred," offered Reinman.

"A thousand."

He said, "Couple people in the Marina Shops you've done copy-writing for, they say you're pretty good."

"I am."

"Seven fifty."

"A thousand."

"Nine hundred." He slapped the desk with the palm of his hand. "My final offer absolutely."

"Sold."

"Good, then we'll shake hands on it and—"

"We'll draw up a letter of agreement."

He stared again. "You don't trust Max Reinman?"

"I've been a free-lance writer four, nearly five, years, Mr. Reinman. Trusting or not trusting has nothing to do . . ."

There was something going on out in the main dance studio. Something that caused shouting, swearing, and thumping.

"What the hell?" Max rose up.

The door of his office slapped open.

Rod Flanders, a fresh cut over his eye, shoved a large, dark man into the office. "You know this bastard?" he asked Reinman.

Sitting back down, Reinman said, "I do."

"What'd I tell you, faggot?" The big man's dark hair was curly, his nose flattened. His suit didn't fit him exactly right, and it was faded and wrinkled. He wore a dress shirt but no tie. "Now take your goddamn hands off me."

"Watch your language, Ernie," warned Reinman.

Ernie Garcia swayed on his feet, turned to take in Jan. "Excuse me, miss," he said, his words somewhat slurred. "Don't mean to offend you. It's just that this faggot grabbed me from behind and—"

"I caught you trying to slip into the locker rooms."

"Like hell," protested Garcia. "I was only just looking for the john."

Reinman said, "This isn't a gym anymore."

"Don't I know that? Shit, I'm not punch-drunk, man."

"It's ladies only around here now," the owner went on. "And I don't want you hanging around, Ernie."

"Who the hell is hanging around? I had to use a toilet, so I come up here," said Garcia. His eyes were bloodshot. "Christ, Max, you got enough money out of me back then."

"Then ain't now."

"Hell, I wasn't doing any—"

"Some of the ladies are awfully upset," said Flanders. "They heard the rumpus when I caught him. If you can handle him, I'd better go back and soothe them."

"Sure, go ahead, Rod."

"Yeah, you flit off and do that, Rodney." Garcia gave a growling laugh.

Shrugging at Jan, Flanders left.

"Maybe we can have our meeting later, Mr. Reinman," the young woman suggested.

"No, we'll have it right now," he said evenly. "Ernie, you maybe got a rough deal and I'm sorry. But I had nothing to do with it and I owe you nothing. Understand, my boy?"

"I didn't come here for any goddamn handout," the ex-boxer said. "Jesus, Max, I just had to take a leak. Honest."

"Yeah, maybe. The point is, Ernie, things change. You're not welcome here no more."

"If I was a faggot like that blond guy out there, then I could—"

"You know I don't like cops much, but if you keep hanging around, I sure as hell am going to call them."

Garcia laughed. "Shit, I don't go anywhere I'm not invited," he said, stumbling as he made his way to the door. "Maybe, though, Max, I'll be back on my feet again sometime. Sometime soon. I'll remember you tossing me out on my can." He bumped the door jamb with his broad shoulder as he staggered out of the office.

Max got up, walked to the doorway to watch the fighter depart. "He wasn't a bad fighter once," he said. "You ever see him in the ring?"

"No," said Jan.

"I guess it was before your time."

Chapter 4

Kevin Wagner seldom knocked.

He came sauntering into his sister's bedroom and lowered his bulky figure down onto the edge of her bed. "Sis, you haven't given me a report on your first day in school."

Lizbeth was at her dressing table, brushing her hair. "It was quite exciting."

"I imagined it would be."

"A crazy man, some sort of nut case, tried to break into the locker rooms while we were dressing," she said. "Gave us all quite a thrill."

"You're joking?" He watched her, eyes narrowing.

"I long ago lost the ability to joke, dear."

"Who was the man, any idea?"

"Some drunken boxer somebody said, former boxer," she answered. "Apparently he worked out there when the place was a gymnasium."

"Is that sort of thing likely to happen every day? I'll phone Reinman and complain about—"

"Nothing serious," she said. "Only a poor drunk."

"I hear they also occasionally have trouble with kid gangs down there. Maybe this wasn't such a good—"

"Oh, but it was. It was a brilliant notion."

"You think so?"

She turned, looked at him. "You knew she was an instructor there."

"Whom are we discussing?"

"Midge."

He grinned. "How is she?"

"Ticked off at you."

"I certainly don't have any hard feelings toward her."

Lizbeth set the hairbrush aside. "What have you been doing?"

"What's Midge say I've been up to?"

"Annoying her."

"Ah, how times change," he said, sighing. "Once a friendly phone call from me would've—"

"The whole thing is over and done, Kev. Leave the poor woman alone."

"I want her back." He stood.

"She'll never come back to you."

"Faith can move mountains."

"But it won't move Midge Branner."

"Is that what she's calling herself again?"

"Wisely, yes."

He shook his head, smiling sadly. "I came to tell you I'm meeting someone for dinner at the yacht club," he said. "You won't mind dining alone here?"

"I prefer it."

He moved to the door. "Will you keep attending the salon?"

"Yes, if only to keep an eye on Midge," said his sister. "And to make certain you stop bothering her."

The night rain hit hard on the flagstones of the patio outside. Connie Sloane shivered once, returning her attention to the screen of the family-room color set.

"That's funny." The seven o'clock news was over and she found herself watching a game show. "Must've dozed off."

She glanced at the wall clock over the wet bar. Nearly ten to eight.

". . . one hundred people surveyed. Top five answers on the board," the television set was saying.

She was always uneasy when Curt was late getting home on bad weather nights. "He's a good driver, but—"

"Connie?"

She brightened, touched her dark hair with her right hand. "I'm in the family room," she called to her husband as she rose from the sofa.

He came hurrying down the three steps into the dark-paneled room. "Mrs. Mott again," he explained, shaking his head. "She wanted her sister, who's from Bel Air and an even nastier bitch than she is, to have a look around the Berrill place with her."

"Is it a sale?"

He kissed her on the cheek, then sat down on the sofa. "Not yet," he said, slumping and loosening his tie while she settled down next to him. "God, the sister had to turn on every faucet in the whole blasted house. She must have some kind of plumbing fixation."

"A house is a big investment."

"Not for that dame. Three-hundred fifty thousand dollars is a spit in the bucket for Mrs. Mott," he said, leaning back. "I'll bet she carries that much around in her purse."

Connie asked him, "Shall I start dinner?"

"In a minute." He shut his eyes, relaxing.

He looked like a schoolboy, slim and youthful. Connie took his hand. "I went to the aerobic dancing class."

Curt opened his eyes. "Hell, I forgot to ask you about it," he said. "How'd it go?"

"Fine. I didn't have any problems keeping up."

"See? I told you." He rubbed the back of his neck. "How many in your class?"

She thought, counting on her fingers. "Eight."

"Anyone you know?"

"Well, not really," she answered. "Although I did meet Jan Early before. She's a free-lance writer and she did a story about our church fair for the *News-Hour* last fall. Pretty girl. And . . . this is sort of interesting . . . Lizbeth Wagner's in the class."

"Who's she?"

"You know, the model. You saw her everywhere a few years ago," Connie said. "She was the Ellison Hi-Fash Jeans girl on TV. Remember?"

"Remember her rear end," he grinned. "She still look like that?"

"She's put on a little weight and she's been ill or . . ."

"Or what?"

"I don't like to talk about people. But I think she's had a drinking problem. She's got that look."

"Too bad."

"Jan was talking about a fairly new vegetarian restaurant in the—"

"Where you can graze on carrots and grass?"

"No, really. It's supposed to be quite good and near the salon. A few of us were thinking of going there for an early dinner some night after class."

"Okay by me. What night?"

"This Thursday maybe?" She looked at him for approval.

"Sure. Just call me at the real estate office first, leave word with Lorrie if I'm out. I'll pick up a pizza or something."

"You won't mind?"

"Not a bit," he assured her. "You like your instructor?"

"Yes, her name's Midge Branner and she's nice. Although . . ."

"Although what?"

"She seemed a bit nervous today. I got the feeling she knew Lizbeth Wagner before and that they didn't exactly like each other," she said. "We may ask Midge to go along to dinner with us."

"Doesn't she work at night there?"

"There aren't any night sessions at the salon yet. Except on Mondays, and a fellow named Rod Flanders handles that one.

He nodded. "So all in all, things turned out okay?"

"They did."

"I knew they would," he said.

Without looking up from the lecture notes spread out before him on the kitchen table, Matt Prize reached out for the chunk of milk chocolate he'd been munching off and on for the past hour. His fingers encountered instead a freshly peeled carrot. "Gad," he muttered, glancing up.

Arms folded, Jan was standing near the table. "You really do concentrate," she said. "A stealthy person like myself could sneak in here and make off with all your worldly goods."

"You could pack just about everything I own into a middle-size shopping bag." Matt pushed back from the table, stretched. "Where'd you hide my chocolate?"

"You're the detective, find it."

"It better not be in the garbage bucket beneath the sink."

"Too obvious." She crossed to the stove. "How much longer you going to be lost in that academic trance?"

"Just about finished." He began gathering up his notes. "How's the brochure coming?"

"Fitfully." She turned on the burner beneath the glass teakettle. "Can I interest you in a cup of peppermint tea?"

"Not at all." He stacked the notebook pages beside his worn briefcase. "How was your aerobic fling this afternoon?"

"Fraught with adventure."

"How so?"

"For one thing, there seems to be a phantom of the salon," answered Jan while fetching a tea bag off a cupboard shelf.

"Cloak and slouch hat?"

"Rumpled suit," she said. "Actually he's just a broken-down fighter. Ernie Garcia, looks to be about forty. Ever heard of him?"

Matt frowned. "Just today, matter of fact. Norm and I were talking about him. Garcia's fresh out of prison."

"Was he in for a crime of violence?"

"Nope, for being part of a gang that looted cargo at the airport." Matt left his chair. "Garcia wasn't the mastermind of the group, but he was the only one they caught."

"I met him, sort of, and he didn't really look like mastermind material," she said. "He was drunk and disorderly."

"What was he doing there?"

"Looking for a bathroom and revisiting his old haunts, or so he claimed."

"What do you think he was really up to?"

She shook her head, watching the lanky Matt walk to the sink and reach to the shelf that held a row of canisters. "I'm not sure what he was up to. But Max Reinman had him hustled out of there fast."

"Is the layout up there the same as it was when the place was a gym?" He lifted the flour canister from its perch.

"The locker and shower areas are. The gym itself's been partitioned, as I understand it."

"Wonder what Garcia really wanted." He removed the lid and reached into the canister. He fished out his hunk of missing chocolate, blew the traces of flour off it.

Jan laughed. "How the heck'd you know I dumped it in there?"

"Flour," he said. "You've got a smear of it on your jeans and on your face. You got some on your hand when you sank my candy."

She inspected her backside. "A bad habit, automatically wiping my hands on myself when they've got flour on them."

"Thus do telltale clues lead us to the culprit." He held the rescued chocolate up. "Proving once again that crime does not pay."

"Eventually I'll outwit you," she promised.

Chapter 5

THURSDAY WAS ANOTHER GRAY DAY.

When Max Reinman came downstairs to the street exit at a few minutes shy of five in the afternoon, a hard, heavy rain was falling. He stood under the Diana Aerobic Salon awning, turning up the collar of his overcoat and gazing forlornly out at the choppy ocean. His car was parked over in a lot at the edge of the Marina, and there wasn't any way he was going to get across the rain-swept street without getting soaked.

"A cold I'll come down with, for sure."

His wife always told him that wet doesn't cause colds; germs and viruses do. Reinman knew better. You get drenched, you get sick. Nine times out of ten.

The lights of the Marina threw multicolored patterns onto the rain slick street. The passing cars hissed and splashed.

"Don't look like it's going to let up. So—"

"Mr. Reinman. Hey, this is terrific."

A lean young man of about twenty was standing beside him under the awning. His dark hair was long, curly. Beads of water dotted his Levi jacket. The smile on his face curled at the edges, showing two cracked and jagged teeth.

"I got nothing to say to you, Kendig."

"That's great, Mr. Reinman," said Jack Kendig. "I can do all the talking then. You can just listen, you know."

"No, I heard all from you—"

"You haven't, Mr. Reinman. Has he?"

Two more young men materialized out of the rain. They were bigger and wider than Kendig. The blond one had a coiled snake tattooed on the back of his right hand. Their smiles were as cold as the afternoon.

"Listen to Jack," advised the one with the snake.

"That's good advice, Mr. Reinman." Kendig took hold of the salon owner's arm. "See, we're really fellow businessmen. Isn't that so?"

"That's so," agreed the one with the snake.

"You better not try anything, Kendig," warned Reinman. "I was running this place when you was still messing your pants. I've tossed bigger hoods than—"

"We're not hoodlums, Mr. Reinman," said Kendig, increasing the pressure on his arm. "No, we're just only, you know, looking out for the welfare of San Amaro. Sort of like those Guardian Angel guys they got back in New York. Except we got more expenses than they do and so we have to charge you something."

"It's cheap," said the one with the snake.

"It is cheap, Mr. Reinman," said Kendig. "Hundred dollars a week and you won't have any trouble."

"I ain't going to pay you a damn thing," Reinman told him. "And I ain't going to have any trouble either. Because if I do—"

"Trouble's funny." Kendig's left hand dropped to his side. When it swung back up there was a jackknife in it. "You never know when it'll hit. Like they say on the TV insurance commercials, you know, it's best to be prepared."

"A hundred's nothing to you," said the one with the snake. "Hell, you'd pay that for just one day in the hospital."

"Listen to me good, Kendig," said Reinman. "You're a punk and you aren't nowhere as tough as you think. You keep pushing and I'll bring in people who—"

"Hey, Mr. Reinman, I wish you didn't call me names."

"Now he's going to have to hurt you," explained the one with the snake.

"I don't think so." Rod Flanders had come quietly down the stairs from above and emerged now onto the sidewalk.

Kendig glanced over at him, grinning. "You're too pretty to scare me," he said, but he put away his knife. "We'll talk again real soon, Mr. Reinman. And, you know, it's not just you who can have an accident. Some of those ladies can, too." He nodded at his two companions.

They backed away into the hard rain.

"Thanks, Rod," said Reinman as he watched them hurry away along the late afternoon sidewalk.

"We ought to go to the police, Maxie."

"Naw, that's not necessary."

"Kendig's roughed up a few people in this area

46

already, business people he's trying to collect protection money from," the instructor said. "We don't want any of our customers hassled."

"These schmucks won't do anything." Reinman pulled out his pocket handkerchief and wiped at his forehead. "Otherwise I'll bring in some muscle of my own."

"Might make things worse."

Shaking his head, Reinman said, "Anyway, I got to get home before my wife starts worrying."

"Want me to walk you to your car?"

"Am I a little old granny? I don't need no escort," he said. "Go back upstairs and take care of business."

"Okay, Maxie. I just came down when I heard what sounded like a fracas."

"I appreciate that," said Reinman. "But try not to call me Maxie."

The proprietor of Lofton's Eden restaurant greeted the four of them at the door. Jan Early he recognized at once. "Miss Early, this is great," he said. "Excuse me if I don't shake hands." He was a slim man of thirty-one, middle-size, his dark hair worn long. His right hand was wrapped round with gauze and white tape.

"What happened, Stew?" asked Jan.

Stew Lofton looked away. "Nothing, just a stupid accident in the kitchen," he said. "Spilled hot safflower oil on myself. Not too smart, huh?"

"I hope you can still cook."

"Sure, and I've got my woman helping out. You know Susan, don't you? Sure, you mentioned her in that great article you wrote about the restaurant."

"We'd like a table for four," said Jan.

"It's early, so you can take your pick. Over in the arbor?"

"That'll be fine," Jan said after looking at the other three women.

Lofton's vegetarian restaurant had fifteen white-clothed tables. There was an artificial grape arbor, left over from the days when this had been a Greek café, taking up a third of the room. There were five additional tables in there.

"Working late tonight, Midge?" Lofton asked as he escorted them across the nearly empty restaurant.

She nodded, smiling down at the denim skirt she was wearing over her dark leotards. "I guess I didn't hide my work clothes well enough."

"Susan had two years of ballet," Lofton said, seating them at a large round table.

"I always wanted to take ballet lessons," said Connie Sloane. "Never did, though."

"You didn't miss anything," said Betsy Grossman, the fourth member of the party. She was an attractive brunette of twenty-five. "I had eight years of that and all I ended up with was bunions up to here."

"Eight years," said Connie. "You must've started very—"

"I began, or rather I was shoved into it, when I was seven years old." Betsy picked up one of the menus Lofton had left before returning to his position at the doorway of the place. "My mother, rest her soul—and I say that even though the old dear is still alive—she was a stage-mother type. A combination of Joan Crawford and what's-her-name who raised Gypsy Rose Whosis. I hated ballet."

"Then why are you taking this aerobic dancing class?" Connie inquired.

"Exercise, pure and simple. I had two children before I was twenty-three." She nodded with determination. "It's time to get back into shape."

"You're very attractive already."

"Attractive maybe, chic no."

Midge was sitting between Connie and Jan. She leaned toward Jan, saying, "You know Lofton well?"

"Casually. I did a piece about their restaurant for *Vegetarian News,* and I have dinner here now and then."

"The thing about his hand," she said, lowering her voice. "It wasn't an accident."

"What do you mean?"

"This isn't something you can write up probably," the instructor said. "But I heard, from Rod Flanders at the salon, that there's a gang making trouble for some of the people who do business around here. Kids mostly."

"Some kind of extortion, you mean?"

"Pay up or have trouble, that's their slogan," she said. "One of these thugs held Lofton while another one poured boiling oil over his hand. As a sample of what happens to those who don't pay."

Jan shuddered. "Did he go to the police?"

"These lovable kids implied they'd hurt his lady if he makes waves," answered Midge. "So he didn't report anything."

"He's paying them?"

"A hundred dollars a week supposedly."

Jan clenched her fist. "That isn't right. Somebody ought to—"

"I didn't bring this up to get you going on a crusade, Jan."

"Yes, but . . . maybe I can talk to someone about it."

"The law?"

"No, a friend of mine. He's a professor of criminology at Cal State." Unclenching her hand, she picked up her menu. "He might have some suggestions."

"I shouldn't even be talking about it," said Midge. "But I never know when to keep my mouth shut. That's how I ended my marriage."

"By talking too much?" asked Betsy.

"No, by telling him what I thought of him. And then adding, 'I'm leaving'."

Betsy looked up from her menu and across at Jan. "The prof you mentioned. He's Matthew Prize, isn't he?"

"Yes."

"Thought so. He lectured our San Amaro Newcomers Club last year. He's . . . very interesting."

"Is that," asked Midge, "better than handsome?"

"He's not a hunk exactly," replied Betsy. "But in his own way, he's very good looking."

Jan smiled. "I'd agree."

"You two," asked Betsy, "are . . . engaged?"

"Just living together," said Jan.

Connie coughed into her hand. "My," she said. "I'm always hearing about people who do that, but I never know any."

"Seems like a fine idea to me," said Midge. "Like taking a test drive before you buy the darn car. Getting married hangs you up with a ton of papers and red tape. I'm still not completely clear of . . . my ex."

"Curt and I never have any trouble," said Connie.

"And we've been married eleven years almost. He's not overpossessive or—"

"But you had to phone him before you could come along tonight," reminded Betsy. "That's like checking in and out with the housemother."

"No, it's simply that I want him to know when I won't be home, so he won't worry," Connie said. "It's a mutual thing."

"I got married at eighteen," said Betsy. "Mostly because Rick seemed like a better deal than my mother." She shrugged. "At least he doesn't insist I take ballet lessons."

"What's he do?" asked Connie.

"I'm not exactly sure. But he works for Wagner Electronics over in Loma Vista and— What's wrong, Midge?"

Midge shook her head. "Nothing," she said checking her watch. "Except I remembered I have to go back up to the salon tonight to work out some routines by myself. So maybe we'd better order."

"Oh, I thought I'd said something that upset you," said Betsy.

"Not at all."

Chapter 6

AFTER THE FOUR SEPARATED OUTSIDE THE restaurant, Midge Branner walked rapidly along the early evening street. The rain was still coming down and the surf was pounding the shore along the Marina. "Fits right in with my mood," she said to herself.

Silly, though, to let things upset her. Just because Betsy Grossman mentioned Kevin's company, that was no reason to go all weak in the knees.

She glanced back over her shoulder, then started up the stairway to the second-floor entrance of the salon. The stairs could do with a few more lights.

Stopping at the top of the stairs, she started to reach into her purse for her keys. Then she noticed the door wasn't quite shut.

Midge opened it, entered the main studio. "Anybody home?" she called out.

The lights were on but the big room was empty. All

she saw were reflections of herself, bounced back and forth between the mirrored walls on the right and left.

Midge walked across the room and dropped her purse down on one of the chairs against the blank wooden wall.

When the door slammed open behind her, she gave a yelp and spun around. "Excuse it," she said, grinning. "Guess I'm jittery."

"My fault," said Rod Flanders. He had on a sport coat and slacks, was carrying a tote bag. "I didn't know you were here, love, and came barging in like the Charge of the Light Brigade."

"What are you up to this late?"

"Working on the account books," he said. Then he nodded at the doorway he'd come through, the one leading to the lockers. "Thought I heard something back there as I was leaving. Guess we're all jittery tonight."

"Anything?"

"No, unless it's mice," answered Flanders. "I spotted some plaster dust in one corner, as though they'd maybe been gnawing at the wall. Have to mention that to Maxie. How was your dinner?"

"Healthful."

He laughed. "You going to be working here all alone?"

"Me and my phonograph, yes."

"Want me to stick around?"

"I'll be okay."

He stood, watching their reflections in the nearest mirrored wall. "Nobody's been bothering you, have they?"

Midge ran her tongue over her upper lip. "Like who?"

"I meant these young hoods who've been giving some of the merchants a bad time," he answered. "They were leaning on Maxie this afternoon."

"Don't tell me he's going to give in and—"

"Not him. But I am a bit concerned. He's an awfully nice man, but not as tough as he was back when this was a gymnasium."

Midge said, "Lofton was at his restaurant tonight. His hand is all bandaged up."

"That's the sort of thing I mean," said Flanders. "I really do think, no matter what Maxie says, I'll have a talk with the police in another day or so. Not that I have much affection for the boys in blue."

"Suppose we both have a serious talk with Max tomorrow," she suggested, undoing the skirt she had on over her dance leotards.

"Good idea, Midge." He patted her on the shoulder. "Just to be on the safe side, I'll lock you in when I leave. Okay?"

"Might as well," she said. "Thanks for your concern."

"We're nearly family," he said and waved goodbye.

Midge put a record on the portable player. It was swing music—an old Count Basie LP, not Top Forty stuff. She liked the beat of it, though.

She had an idea for a new aerobic dance routine and . . .

Frowning, the young woman bit her lower lip.

Turning down the volume of the music, Midge walked to the door that led to the locker-room and shower area.

She pushed the door open, stood listening and looking down the dim-lit corridor. All she heard was the rain hitting on the roof overhead.

"Somebody back here?" she said, not really loudly enough to be heard from very far off.

"Now, don't go doing anything stupid. Don't walk in on something."

She had a feeling, sensed it, that there'd been some motion back here. Maybe she'd even heard something, a faint tapping sound.

Swallowing once, Midge walked down the hall. She took slow careful steps as she made her way to the locker room.

She hesitated on the threshold. Several scents mixed. Dampness, perfume, soap.

Count Basie's band was still playing back in the dance studio, sounding very far away.

Midge entered the room. There were two rows of green metal lockers. Two dozen lockers against each wall. Then you went along a short, tile-floored passageway and you were in the showers.

She cleared her throat, taking a slow careful look around the locker room. Near one of the benches in front of a row of lockers someone had dropped a hair barrette.

Midge walked over, bent from the waist and picked it up. There was a dusting of white powder on it.

She looked up at the plaster wall and noticed a small hole about six feet up and near a support beam.

That wasn't there before, was it?

Midge thrust two fingers into the hole and poked around.

Thunder sounded close by. The lockers seemed to rattle.

"Gee!" She pulled her fingers free, blew the plaster dust off them. Her heart was fluttering.

Dumb to let a little thunder scare you.

She turned away from the back wall.

Then she wished she hadn't.

Midge saw the foot then. The toe of a tennis shoe really. There was someone standing in the shower room. Someone who felt hidden, but wasn't.

When she first noticed the foot, she made a gasping sound.

That wasn't too smart.

"Okay," said Midge inside her head. *"This is no time for any more foolishness. Let's just get the hell out of here. Casually. Pretending we didn't see a damn thing."*

She even tried to whistle, but gave up on that.

She made it across the locker room.

Her back felt suddenly cold. As though it had turned to ice and would shatter if something so much as tapped it.

In the corridor. Safe so far.

Don't run.

Don't panic.

One step, then another.

Count the steps maybe. That'll take your mind off whoever it is who's lurking back there.

Fifteen.

Sixteen.

Seventeen.

Never knew this corridor was so long.

More thunder, and the rain pounding down.

The door was only about five steps away now.

Out in the dance studio Jimmy Rushing had started singing.

". . . sent for you yesterday, and here you come today . . ."

Midge opened the door.

All she had to do was get across the studio and then she could double-time down the stairs to the street.

She took three steps before someone grabbed her.

". . . sent for you yesterday, and here you come today . . ."

Rod Flanders decided to go back.

After leaving the salon he'd gone over to Lofton's Eden for dinner. Seeing Lofton's injured right hand, talking to him about Jack Kendig had started Flanders worrying.

He ate quickly, then hurried back to the Diana Aerobic Salon.

The rain hadn't let up much and a nasty wind was blowing in off the dark Pacific.

While he was still a block from the place, he saw someone coming out of the salon stairwell. A woman with long dark hair, wearing a plaid raincoat. She walked off in the opposite direction.

Flanders couldn't place her, didn't recognize her, at this distance anyway, as one of the Diana customers.

Halfway up the stairs he became aware of the phonograph. The record was stuck in a groove; a gruff-voiced singer kept repeating, "Sent for you yesterday, and here you come today . . ."

Flanders ran up the steps.

He grabbed the door-knob, turned it and found the door locked. He fumbled out his keys, unlocked the door and went in.

". . . sent for you yesterday, and here you come today . . ."

He saw her at once, lying there far across the room. On her side, back to him. Huddled like a sleeping child.

Except there was blood all around. Smeared over her tunic top, staining the floor in angry red blotches.

"Jesus!" He shook his head, not wanting to believe what he saw.

Then he ran to Midge, aware of the images of himself in the mirrored walls. His anxious figure multiplied and multiplied.

And the image of the dead woman repeated over and over.

He knew she was dead. Never had any doubt of it.

When he reached her, knelt down, and saw that she'd been stabbed again and again, he simply nodded.

He found he was having trouble breathing. His mouth was open, he was gasping in air. Reaching down, he touched Midge's cheek. Her flesh was still warm but it had the feel of death to it.

"Poor kid," he said aloud. "Poor kid."

When he got to his feet, he almost fell. He felt dizzy all at once.

"Jesus, get hold of yourself."

He looked around the room, noticing now that there was no sign of a knife.

". . . sent for you yesterday, and here you come today . . ."

Although he knew you weren't supposed to touch anything, he moved to the portable phonograph and lifted the needle off the old LP. Then it occurred to him that the person who'd killed Midge might still be here.

Well, he didn't intend to panic.

He walked deliberately to Max Reinman's office and opened the door. Leaving it open wide, he went in.

He reached across the desk, picked up the phone. It was working; he got a humming dial tone. He let out his breath and dialed the local emergency number.

"Yes?" said a female voice after a half minute.

"I don't know exactly how to go about this," said Flanders, "but I want to report a murder."

Chapter 7

MATT PRIZE WAS BREWING HIMSELF A CUP OF hot cocoa when the wall phone rang. He lowered the heat under the pan of milk, sprinted to the phone. It was probably Jan.

"Hello."

"Am I interrupting some blissful domestic interlude?" asked Norm Levine.

"Jan's out. Fact is I thought you were her phoning." The clock next to the phone showed 9:15 P.M. "What's happening?"

"Remember at our lavish lunch the other day we were chatting about the Diana Aerobic Salon," said the reporter. "Well, I'm on my way over there now."

"Something wrong?"

"Been a killing. Editor just called to tell me to cover the—"

"Who was killed, do you know?"

"You sound concerned. Is there—"

"Jan was having dinner down in that area, with some of the women from her class."

"Far as I know this is one of the instructors, a lady," said Norm. "Didn't mean to unsettle you. Now then, old chum, would you care to meet me there? You've lent the local minions of the law a helping hand in the past and—I'll admit a crass and selfish motive—it's always made damned good copy for my yarns in the respected pages of the *News-Hour*."

"Yeah, I am interested." Matt looked toward the window. He could see the garage and driveway. "Who's on the case?"

"Your old crony Lieutenant Phil Redding."

"We get along."

"Hell, you ought to, after you helped him clear up that computer-tapping murder business last—"

"I'll get over there soon as I can," he promised. "Anybody have any idea of who might've done the killing?"

"Nope, the field is wide open," answered his friend. "Which is one of the reasons I summoned you. An exclusive solution'll make for a terrific story."

"Sometimes, if I didn't know you were such a decent fellow down deep, I'd suspect your motives. 'Bye."

After hanging up, Matt turned off the burner. He went into the cottage's small living room, retrieved his brown loafers from where he'd abandoned them next to his armchair.

The mantel clock read 9:23.

"Where the hell is she?"

There'd been a murder at the salon. It might even have happened while Jan . . .

He straightened up, grinning.

He'd heard her old British sports car come rattling up their gravel driveway.

"Too much imagination's a liability in this trade," he reminded himself.

Snagging a tweed jacket out of the hall closet, Matt headed out the back door. He reached the carport just as Jan was swinging out of the parked car.

"You okay?" he asked her.

"Nice of you to ask. But eating at a natural foods restaurant isn't likely to endanger my—"

"Listen, Jan." He took hold of her hand. "There's been some trouble down at Reinman's place. I have—"

"Those damn kids. What did they—"

"Which kids?"

"Gang of young toughs. They've been— Did they vandalize the salon or what?"

"How many instructors does Reinman have?"

"Only two. Midge Branner . . . you know, she's the one who came to dinner with us tonight . . . and Rod Flanders."

"When'd you see her last, this Midge?"

"About 6:30 I guess. She left early and the rest of us sat around talking for another half hour before . . . Matt . . . has something happened to Midge?"

He nodded slowly. "Looks like," he said. "She's dead."

"Oh, no." She slumped against him.

"I'm going down there. You be okay here?"

"What . . . what happened?"

"Not sure yet. But, from what Norm told me on the phone, she was murdered."

"But we were just . . ." She gave an angry shake of

her head. "Oh, hell, that's what people always say when someone dies. 'I just saw him yesterday . . . I talked to her on the phone this morning.' But, my God, Matt, Midge was alive only a few hours ago. Are you certain it is Midge?"

"He didn't give me the name, but he knows it's a woman instructor. Sounds like it has to be Midge Branner."

"Maybe not, though. Maybe it's . . . a perfect stranger who just happened to be there."

"Jan, that's not likely."

"No, I suppose not." She rested her head against his chest. "I'm coming along."

"The police won't let you in."

"I'll wait in the car for you. I know I'm not staying here."

He took the keys from her hand. "We'll take your car. Scoot around to the passenger seat."

After a few seconds she stepped back from him, wiping at her eyes with a thumb knuckle. "She wasn't much older than I am."

Matt put his arm around Jan's shoulders and guided her around the front of the low gray car. "We can talk about her on the way over."

"You'll do something about this, won't you, Matt?" she asked as she sank into the bucket seat. "Find out who did it?"

"Sure going to try," he said.

The left windshield wiper was making a slippery, snickering sound. Now and then drops of night rain got in through the venerable canvas top of Jan's old car.

"How'd she seem tonight?" Matt was asking as he guided the car along the tree-lined lanes of this residential stretch of San Amaro. The rain-filled wind rattled the leaves of the pepper trees.

"Midge was . . . she was preoccupied with something." Jan sat, hugging herself, watching the headlights cut into the rain.

"Any idea what?"

"She told me these young hoodlums had approached Max Reinman tonight; maybe that was it. They threatened him with trouble if he didn't pay up."

Matt said, "I wonder if they'd go as far as murder."

"They're mean. Stew Lofton, he runs the restaurant we ate at tonight, they burned his hand quite badly. Poured hot oil on it."

"Lofton tell you about it?"

"No, Midge did."

"Had these kids made any specific threats?"

"Not that I know of."

"Who else was with you two at dinner?"

"Betsy Grossman . . . oh, that was something odd."

"What?"

"Betsy was talking about her husband . . . Rick I think his name is. When she mentioned where he worked, Midge practically did a double take. As though the name really upset her. Then she pretended nothing was wrong."

"Which company?"

"Wagner Electronics."

"Was it the name of the company or the mention of Betsy's husband that bothered Midge?"

Jan considered. "No, it was Wagner Electronics."

"Who else was with you?"

"Just Connie Sloane. Poor Connie."

"Why poor?"

"She's . . . well, about as far from a liberated

woman as you can get," replied Jan. "She's taking this aerobic dancing class because her husband told her she ought to. And she was really nervous tonight about phoning her husband, making sure he knew she was going to dinner and where and with whom."

"That's just being thoughtful. Would that more people were."

"I stopped at the library on my way home. Thursday is the night it's open till nine. I had to look up something more about aerobic dancing, for the darned brochure."

"What does Connie's husband do?"

"Real estate. Not too successfully either."

"She tell you that?"

"Oh, not directly. But when we chat around the locker room and the girls talk about vacations or new cars or whatever, why, Connie always explains that she and Curt decided not to take a vacation this year and that they don't really need a new second car and so on."

He grinned. "You're getting spoiled by our Southern Cal affluence."

"Sure, by the affluence we can amass by pooling your prof's salary with the princely sums I get from *Vegetarian News*."

"Had Midge been talking about anything—or anybody—else that was bothering her?"

"Not to me, but . . ." She frowned, thinking back. "The first day of class, after it was over, I think she had some kind of spat with one of the girls. With the illustrious Lizbeth Wagner in fact."

"About what?"

"Wasn't close enough to hear."

"Midge married?"

"Not now. She's divorced, or at least separated."

"Her husband in the area?"

"I'm not certain, but I think maybe yes."

Matt turned onto the road that would lead them into the business district of San Amaro. "Would Lizbeth Wagner be related to Wagner Electronics?"

Jan looked over at him. "Gosh, I don't know. But they must be, huh?"

"Midge had an argument with Lizbeth Wagner; she was upset at the mention of the Wagner company," he said. "Something to follow up."

Jan steepled her fingers, rested her chin on them. "It could be just some madman who broke in there," she said. "Just a chance piece of violence."

"Most murders don't happen that way," Matt told her. "There's always a reason."

Chapter 8

THEY WERE BRINGING MIDGE'S BODY OUT just as Matt and Jan came driving past the salon. One of the white-coated paramedics slipped on the wet sidewalk and the front end of the stretcher nearly dropped from his grasp. The rain pelted at the shrouded body as the two men carried it to the waiting ambulance; the wind worried at a dangling stretcher strap.

There were two police cars double-parked to the rear of the ambulance, roof lights pulsing. Every space along that side of the block was filled and there were at least two dozen people gathered on the sidewalk. A local TV news truck was stopped half up on the curb and a husky black man was unloading video equipment. His partner tried to shield him with a big umbrella the wind wanted to wrest away.

"Swing around and stop near the entrance," suggested Jan. "You can hop out while I find a space."

"Guess you'll have to." Matt executed a U-turn, pulling the old sports car up alongside the news wagon. "See you soon."

"Be careful." She climbed over into the driver's seat once he'd stepped out into the rainy night.

Waving, Matt sprinted to the sidewalk. He dodged the curious locals and made his way to the entrance.

"Everybody stay back," the young uniformed policeman was ordering. "Nobody can— Oh, good evening, Mr. Prize."

"Hi. Tad. Is Lieutenant Redding up there?"

Tad McCrae nodded. He was a tall, red-haired young man of twenty-six. He was proud of his military-style mustache and he touched it now. "I suppose it's okay to let you up, since you and the lieutenant are friends. And you've sort of helped him out on cases before." He pointed toward the stairway with his thumb. "Go on up, sir."

"In a minute." The canvas awning kept the rain off them. "Like to talk to you first."

Patrolman McCrea smiled, smoothing his mustache. "Glad to help."

"Who found the body?"

"That instructor here, Rod Flanders." His forehead creased.

"You don't like the guy?"

"Well, I shouldn't say that," answered McCrea. "See, I believe a police officer should be free of prejudice. And just because this guy is gay as a fruitcake, I shouldn't automatically not like him. So I'm trying to be noncommittal."

"Succeeding?"

"About sixty percent."

"You the first officer on the scene?"

He nodded in the direction of one of the prowl cars. "Rogers and Yoe got the call and beat me here. See, this is my beat on foot. When I saw them heading up there, I tagged along."

"How was she killed?"

McCrea shook his head, swallowing, looking uneasy. "You've got to get used to this sort of thing, if you're going to be an effective officer, but . . . damn, it was pretty bad," he said. "She was knifed. Breasts and stomach . . . all. It was bad."

"Weapon up there?"

"They haven't found it yet, if it is. Least they hadn't when I got sent down here to keep out tourists."

"I hear there's been some trouble with kid gangs hereabouts." Matt looked toward the street and saw Jan easing her car into a space across the way. "You notice any of them hanging around tonight?"

"I know who you mean. See, if we could get the merchants around here to come in and swear out complaints then . . . but, no, I didn't see Jack Kendig and his gang around."

"That's his name?"

"Yeah, that's him. Jack Kendig, about twenty. He's a . . . I try to keep an open mind. But Kendig's a scumbag and I don't see how you could rehabilitate him if you had ninety-nine years and a million dollars," the young patrolman said. He hesitated, studying his shoes.

"Anything else?"

"Well, since I already told the lieutenant this, I guess he'll be telling you, sir," McCrea said. "I think maybe I saw the killer."

Matt said, "You did?"

"I'm not sure, you know. But, see, about a quarter to six or so I was going by across the street and I noticed a woman walk up and climb these stairs."

"So you didn't get a close look?"

"No, I was over there in front of the Marina and with the rain and all." He shook his head. "She was dark haired, not too heavy. Had on a plaid raincoat and, I think, a pair of dark sweat pants. Running shoes. At the time I figured she was just another student. Except now it turns out there weren't any classes tonight. So who was she?"

"It couldn't have been Midge Branner you saw?"

"Midge is . . . she was smaller, and I know her special way of walking. No, this wasn't Midge." His face turned grim. "Midge was a pretty lady and I was thinking . . . you know, sometime I'd ask her to have coffee."

"Yeah." Matt waved at Jan in the car. "I'll go on up now, Tad. Thanks."

"Any time, Mr. Prize."

Just inside the door of the salon Matt was met by Norm Levine. The curly-haired reporter caught him by the arm, hauled him over into a corner. "Slight problem she has arisen," he said.

"I see him."

Out in the center of the room Lieutenant Redding, a tall, raw-edged man of forty-one, was in conversation with a short angry-looking man some ten years his senior. As they talked Redding fished a crumpled pack of cigarettes from his suit-coat pocket, shook one out and put it between his lips.

"Mayor Gonzer is unhappy," explained Norm.

"Next you'll tell me it's raining outside."

"Excuse my redundancy, sahib."

Matt scanned the room, noticing the marks on the floor and the bloody smears that indicated where the body of Midge Branner had been sprawled. There were a half dozen other policemen in the salon, plainclothes and uniformed, and two other reporters. An attractive red-haired woman in a jade green pants suit was standing a few feet from the lieutenant and the selectman, waiting with a microphone in her hand. The cord snaked across the wooden floor to a cluster of equipment being watched over by a fat young man. The cameraman who worked with the woman reporter was shooting footage of a couple of plainclothesmen who were hunched over the spot where the girl had fallen.

"What's the target of Gonzer's ire this evening?" Matt asked.

"His Holiness thinks the police have been turning crimes of violence into sideshows," said Norm. "Too much press, too much TV. It lacks dignity."

"He doesn't like me either."

"Hell, he didn't like you back when you were a simple, godfearing gumshoe and he was just a local shyster lawyer."

"True. So it doesn't appear I'll be able to do much nosing around tonight."

"Redding agrees. He passed the word to me to tell you to drop in at his office *mañana*. At nine in the A.M. if possible."

"My first class isn't until eleven. I can make it."

"My photographer—you know, Flashgun Feldman—he got some dandy pictures of the body. I'll get you a set."

"Somebody stabbed her, huh?"

Norm blinked. "How'd you figure that out?"

"McCrea downstairs told me."

"I never get used to seeing stuff like that," said Norm. "And I'm as hardened as they come. It was grim, old chum."

"The other instructor found her?"

"Rod Flanders," said Norm, indicating a half-open door across the salon. "He's in giving a statement to Detective Andreas. I imagine it'll take awhile, since Andreas'll have to look up just about every word."

"Where's Max Reinman?"

"En route. They sent for him to drop in."

"Where was he?"

"Home. Alone."

Matt said, "McCrea says he saw a woman coming in here a bit before six."

"Oh?"

"Don't put that in your story yet."

"Okay, but, darn, I like that angle."

"Wait until Redding gives it to you."

"Who Is the Mystery Woman? Is the Lady in Red the Mad Killer? Those are the headlines that sell papers."

"Lady in plaid in this instance."

"I like red better, and black is best. One of the students?"

"McCrea didn't recognize her. He's sure it wasn't Midge Branner, though."

"But not sure if this lady got here before or after Midge came back?"

"Nope."

Norm said, "I hear the door was locked, when Flanders got here."

Matt looked back at the door he'd used coming in.

"That's not much of a lock," he observed. "You could spring it with a plastic credit card."

"Not me. I don't have the skill, nor do I have any more credit cards," said the reporter. "They keep taking them away from me for the most trivial reasons. Arrears they call it. Did I ever tell you about the time the American Express folks chopped up my card while—"

"Gonzer is scowling my way," mentioned Matt. "Think it's time to withdraw gracefully. Evening, Mr. Mayor."

"May all your piles develop piles," mouthed Norm while the red-faced official was looking their way. "Got time for a beer, Matthew?"

"Jan's waiting down in the car for me," he said, turning toward the doorway. "I'll get in touch with you tomorrow."

When Matt reached the street, he saw Jan standing a few yards away. She was sharing an umbrella with a slightly plump, dark-haired woman and a slender, light-haired man.

"Matt," called Jan, "over here."

"Keep fighting 'em off," Matt advised Patrolman McCrea as he passed him.

"Doing my best, sir."

Jan caught hold of Matt's sleeve and pulled him closer. "This is Connie Sloane and her husband Curt," she said. "This is Matthew Prize."

He shook hands with Sloane, who had a strong grip. "How'd you hear about this?"

"It was on the radio," Curt Sloane answered. "I happened to be listening while I was driving home. Told Con about it and she insisted—"

"I wanted to drive down," his wife said, brushing at

her eyes. "I know there's nothing anyone can do and yet . . . It was just a gesture I guess."

Sloane asked Matt. "Do they have any idea what happened to the poor girl?"

"Not as yet."

"Did somebody break in? One of those punks?"

"It doesn't look that way."

"What sort of safety precautions do they have at this place? How easy is it to get in and out?"

"Wouldn't be too difficult."

Sloane nodded a few times. "I've never been up there. But I think now I should've come in with Connie when she signed up and taken a good look around," he said. "Something like this could happen to anybody and you kick yourself afterward for not having checked out the setup thoroughly. Any house I handle, I make certain all the locks are—"

"We don't really know what happened," said Connie. "After all, it could be some sort of domestic thing."

Matt asked, "Did Midge talk about having that kind of trouble?"

"Well, at dinner tonight she made a few bitter remarks about divorce and all. It was my impression she—"

"I think we've done about all we can here, Con," her husband cut in. "No use standing around in the rain and gossiping about the dead."

"I suppose not. I'm sorry."

Jan took Matt's arm. "Car's right across the street," she said. "Night, Connie. Nice meeting you, Curt."

"Same here."

When they were in the sports car, with Matt at the wheel, Jan said, "Well?"

"Didn't learn much." He started the engine. "Mostly because our esteemed Mayor was on the scene. He has no use for amateur sleuths or members of the fourth estate."

"Gonzer," she said, as though mentioning something sour. "The fact he's actually been elected twice takes away some of your faith in democracy."

Chapter 9

FRIDAY THE SUN WAS BACK. ROBINS WERE hopping around on the grass of the town square. Lieutenant Phil Redding was sitting behind his battered desk with his chair turned so that he could watch the morning square down below. "We don't have much," he said, puffing on his cigarette.

Matt was in a lopsided straight-backed chair. "Can you tell me what you do have?"

Redding coughed. "Did you ever smoke?"

"Not since college."

"How'd you quit?"

"Just decided to stop."

"Hell, I've decided that at least six times this year already." He snuffed out the cigarette in a small pie-pan ashtray. "Okay, Matt. Everything isn't in yet, but I'll fill you in on what I do know."

"You sure this isn't going to arouse the mayor's wrath?"

"Gonzer knows where he can stick his wrath," said the lieutenant. "I'm sorry I had to ignore you up there last night."

"You find a weapon yet?"

"No, looks like he took it with him."

"He?"

"Figure of speech. Might be a woman, we'll come to that."

"Then she wasn't raped or sexually assaulted?"

"No." The policeman shook out a fresh cigarette. "Preliminary tests indicate she wasn't touched in that way."

"Anything stolen from the salon?"

"Not according to Max Reinman. He keeps a couple hundred bucks in cash in a tin box in his desk. That's still there."

Matt asked, "How'd your killer get in?"

"There's no sign of a break-in, but as you probably noticed Reinman's locks wouldn't keep out the most simpleminded burglar. And there's no alarm system at all."

"How exactly was she killed?"

"The killer came at her from behind. He grabbed her around the throat with his left arm while stabbing her in the chest and stomach with a knife held in his right hand." Redding lit his cigarette and then tapped a report on his desk. "The bruises on her throat and the angle of the wounds tell us that."

"She was stabbed quite a few times, wasn't she?"

"Twenty-three."

"That might," suggested Matt, "indicate passion. Or madness."

"Or just plain panic. Hard to say this early."

"She was killed where she was found, in the main dancing studio?"

"Yep, right next to her phonograph."

Matt asked, "Why was Midge Branner there at all? As I understand it, they only have evening classes on Mondays."

"She seems to have been very enthusiastic about her work. Liked to go back after hours some nights to practice new aerobic dancing routines," Redding told him. "I wonder if that aerobic stuff really works."

"Give it a try."

"You've never seen me dance."

Matt said, "People knew she went back there evenings. So somebody wanting to find her alone could count on her being at the salon fairly often."

"That's so, Matt, but the lady also lived alone. You could catch her there, too."

"This guy Flanders found the body?"

Redding fluttered his left hand in the air, shaking ashes loose. "The guy's a swish, but seems to be clean otherwise."

"Being gay isn't a crime anymore."

"Nope, but it indicates, to me anyway, a certain quirkiness," said Lieutenant Redding, taking a long drag on the cigarette. "And maybe I'm looking for somebody who's a bit strange on this one."

"Why did Flanders go up there when he did?"

"He went back because he was concerned about the girl."

"Worried about something specific?"

"He'd run into her when he was leaving. He apparently stays late some nights to do the bookkeeping," said Redding. "And earlier some of our finest local hoods had threatened Max Reinman. Flanders tells me he was worried they might break in and try to hurt Midge Branner. He went back."

"Do you think these kids are capable of murder?"

"I think anybody's capable," answered the lieutenant. "And I've got a pickup order out on the leader, scummy kid named Jack Kendig. I want to have a chat with him."

"What about Flanders himself as a suspect?"

"He was having dinner at that vegetarian joint near there at the time we figure she was killed. Although it's still possible he killed her either before he went out or after he came back. You can't ever pinpoint the time of death that fine."

"I know," said Matt. "But you don't think he did it?"

Redding shrugged. "We're looking into his background. I try to do as little thinking as possible until I have all the facts. Saves wear and tear on the brain." He squinted at the burning end of the cigarette, then poked it into the ashtray.

"Did Flanders see anyone coming or going?"

After coughing a few times into his fist, Redding answered, "He says he saw a woman leaving the salon just as he was getting back there. Brunette in a plaid raincoat."

"One of their customers?"

"He's not sure, since she was half a block or so away."

"You're talking to all the ladies enrolled with Reinman's salon?"

"That's being done even as we speak."

"Tad McCrea saw a lady going in a little before six."

"Probably the same lady, yes," said Redding.

"But you don't know anything else about her?"

"We know she's of medium build and not on the heavy side, and that she likes the color navy blue."

Matt sat up. "How?"

"She left a pair of warm-up pants behind."

"In the dance studio?"

"Nope, back in the locker room," replied the lieutenant. "The reason we're fairly certain they're hers is that they're stained with blood."

"Whose blood?"

"We're checking that out right now."

Matt scratched at his chin. "It'd be possible to get blood on her trousers if she attacked Midge Branner from behind."

"Sure, when you grab someone that way, it's fairly common to hook your right leg in front of their legs," said Redding. "To keep them from kicking you."

"Was most of the blood on the right leg of the sweat pants?"

"It was."

"Can you trace the pants?"

"Doubtful. They happen to be a cheap brand you can buy at all sports shops and most of the department stores *and* discount outlets. Hundreds of pairs get sold in this area each and every year. There are a lot of amateur lady jocks. But we'll see what we can run down on it."

"Men can wear warm-up pants, too."

"This pair has a bright pink strip down each leg," said Redding. "A guy might look a bit fetching in them."

Matt left his chair. He walked over to the other window of the lieutenant's third-floor office. A shaggy black dog was deftly dodging the traffic down on Main Street and aiming for the sanctuary of the square. "Men in her life?"

"Nobody serious, far as we've been able to find out so far."

"What about her ex-husband?"

Redding chuckled. "You've been doing your homework."

"Jan was in that class."

"I know, and we'll be talking with her sometime today. I may do that myself, see if I can persuade her to dump you," the policeman said. "Did Midge Branner happen to complain about her ex in front of Jan?"

"Not directly. Who is he, the Wagner Electronics heir?"

"Bingo. Yep, it's lovable Kevin Wagner himself."

"And where was he last night?"

"Out and around," replied Redding. "He hasn't got anything in the way of the alibi. Professes to be broken up over her death, was hoping to get back together and so on. He's offered to pay any and all funeral expenses."

"She have any other near relatives?"

"Nobody local. Her landlord thinks there's maybe an aunt back in Boston."

"Did Midge and Wagner part friends?"

Redding laughed. "Nobody parts friends with Kevin Wagner," he said. "He simply isn't a nice guy at all, Matt. Fact is, we have had a couple of complaints about him in the past few months. He has a habit of punching people in fashionable saloons. But with his money and his lawyers, he has yet to spend any time in a cell."

"Big husky guy, isn't he?"

"Fat is how I'd sum up the Wagner scion. Fat and nasty."

"You know his sister was in Midge's class, too?"

"We know and we'll be inquiring about that," answered the lieutenant. "Max Reinman gave us the list of all his customers. Did you know he makes more money with that place now than he did when it was a gym? Incredible."

Matt wandered back to his chair. "What about Ernie Garcia?"

"Just graduated from Las Cruzes Prison."

"And been seen hanging around the Diana Aerobic Salon."

"Yeah, both Max and Flanders mentioned the lad."

"Talked with him?"

"Can't find him. He's got an apartment down on Palma Street, job at a laundry near there. He's not especially visible at either location."

"He's another fellow who can be nasty when he's drunk, as I recall."

"We'll be discussing all that and more with Ernie when we run him to ground."

"What about that gang that was looting shipments out at the airport?"

"Defunct, far as we know."

Matt rubbed at his chin again. "Yet a short while after Ernie gets out, there's a murder at one of his old hangouts."

"It's a dance salon these days, not a gym. They give Ernie the heave-ho whenever he drops in."

Matt stood. "I don't believe in coincidences."

"Not that fond of them myself," said Redding. "Thing is, I am also against jumping at conclusions.

Right now I just don't know enough and, unless you're holding back, neither do you. It's too damn early to make up a theory, without risking bending the facts to fit it. So at the moment I am doing my sponge act, soaking up every damn bit of information I can."

"Is it okay with you if I look around the salon?"

"All the classes are canceled for today, but Max and Flanders ought to be over there," Redding said. "And Officer McCrea is keeping an eye on the place."

"I'll drop over and browse around."

"Go ahead, Matt, but share any insights with me."

"I'll add 'em to your sponge," he promised and left.

There was no one in the main dance studio but a handsome blond young man in street clothes. He was standing, shoulders slumped and hands in trouser pockets, staring down at the place where Midge Branner had fallen. When he heard Matt Prize's footfalls, he looked over at him. "Press?"

Matt shook his head.

From the half-open door of Reinman's office came the sound of conversation.

"He's got three of them in there now," explained the blond young man. "Out of town papers are starting to send people. It's awfully depressing, really, the freak-show aspects of all this." He held out his hand. "I'm Rod Flanders."

Shaking hands, Matt said, "Matt Prize."

"Ah, of course. You're Jan's detective."

"Is that how she refers to me?"

"Certainly not, Matt. She's a very bright young woman. I envy you," Flanders said.

"Lieutenant Redding gave me permission to come over and look around, if that's okay."

"Oh, certainly. We want all the help we can get," the instructor said. "Has someone hired you to look into this?"

"I'm not a licensed private investigator anymore," Matt told him. "I'm just curious."

"Well, I hope you can find out who did it. I keep thinking if I hadn't left the poor kid alone, she—"

"You had no way of knowing, did you?"

Frowning, Flanders answered, "Not really. I mean, no. Except I had a sort of gut feeling, a premonition, that something bad was going to happen."

"How come?"

"I suppose you've heard about those dreadful hoodlums who've been raising hell in the neighborhood. Yes, well, they tried to threaten Maxie last night," he said. "I scared them off, but . . . I don't know, I'm wondering if they didn't come back here and do this awful thing to Midge."

"This is only a feeling, though?"

"Jack Kendig, the ring leader, pulled a knife on Max," said Flanders. "And Midge was stabbed with . . . I suppose you're used to seeing someone dead, but . . . God, it was so awful."

"Nobody ever really gets used to it, Flanders."

"Probably not. It was . . . well, no use dwelling on it. That won't do her any good."

"Did you talk to her when you were leaving last night?"

"Small talk, yes," he answered. "And I told her about Kendig and the other rowdies."

"And the small talk was about what?"

Flanders thought. "Well, she'd been having dinner with some of our ladies . . . you know that, since Jan was one of them. We talked about that," he said. "And . . . oh, yes. This is trivial, but I mentioned I suspected we had mice back in our locker room."

"What gave you that idea?"

"I'd heard scratching noises, then I spotted some plaster dust. As though some little creature had been—"

"Rod, can you scoot in here for a minute?" called Max Reinman. "These people got some questions for you."

"Coming, Maxie." He patted Matt on the arm. "You'll have to excuse me while I go bolster his sagging morale." Flanders hurried into the office.

Matt squatted, surveying the place on the floor where the young woman had died. You could still see traces of blood.

"Is that where it happened?" Curt Sloane had come up and was standing there.

"Apparently so."

The lean, real estate man said, "I've come down to have a talk with Reinman."

"He seems to be holding a press conference at the moment."

Sloane shook his head. "What a world it is. Spill a little blood and everybody wants to read about it," he said. "Well, I decided this place isn't safe. I intend to cancel Connie's agreement with Reinman and get our money back. I wasn't too hot for my wife to take this damned course anyway. It's in a lousy neighborhood really, and it's expensive. But try to tell Connie that, she's eager to sample all the fads. Especially if they promise to lose you weight. All you really have to do to lose weight—but she doesn't believe me—is eat sensibly and exercise. She sure doesn't need to build up her muscles. She can beat me at arm wrestling, and I exercise too!"

"You'll probably have to wait awhile before you can see Reinman."

Sloane consulted his wristwatch. "I have to show a house in about a half hour," he said. "That's a nice place you're renting. We had it listed with us when it was put on the market a few years back."

"Yep, I like it." Matt was glancing around the room. "I didn't get to look around the locker room when I was here last time."

"That doesn't sound like much fun, since there aren't any ladies here today."

"I'm just curious."

"I'll take a look with you, kill the time while I'm waiting for Reinman." Crossing the dance floor, he pushed a door open. "Really distasteful the way people can get publicity even out of death."

Matt followed and they walked along a corridor.

Opening another door, Sloane said, "Here we are."

Matt halted just across the threshold. "Looks like they didn't do much renovating back here."

"Did you come here when this was a gym?"

"No. You?"

"I do all my exercise at home," said Sloane. He sat on one of the benches and sniffed at the air. "I'm into weight lifting, push-ups, sit-ups and so on. You do any of that?"

"Only a little running." Going over to the shower room, Matt looked inside. He noticed a smear of mud on the tile floor near the far wall. The police must've noticed that, too.

Turning, Matt went down the rows of lockers to the back wall.

"You looking for something in particular?" inquired Sloane.

"Don't know exactly what I am looking for."

"You used to be a private eye."

"Never called myself that, but I was one."

"Did that pay well?"

"Relatively so."

"Sure, I suppose you can count on there always being people who don't pay for their cars, and husbands who are jealous and so on," said the real estate man. "It's not like housing, where it's feast or famine."

Matt found a spot on the wall where there was a small hole. He took a pencil out of his inner breast pocket, poked it in the hole. The tip of the pencil didn't strike anything.

"What's that?" Sloane came over to watch.

"Probably a rat hole," answered Matt, although he could see the plaster had been poked at with some sort of sharp tool.

"Another reason to get my wife out of this." Sloane checked his watch once more. "Well, doesn't look like I can wait any longer. You ready to go?"

"Going to poke around a bit more."

"I'll see you around then. We'll have lunch sometime," said Sloane, smiling. "And if you're ever in the mood to buy a house, let me help you."

"That won't be for a while."

Sloane shook hands and left the locker room.

Matt stood gazing at the wall. This part of the building had been barely touched when Reinman converted it from gymnasium to dance studio. Meaning that this wall had been here for several years at least.

"But why is someone poking around here now?" he asked himself. "And did they find what they were looking for?"

Chapter 10

NORM LEVINE WAS IN A SELF-IMPROVEMENT mood. So he walked the six blocks between the *News-Hour* offices and the Diana Aerobic Salon. The clock in the town hall tower was sounding eleven when he came strolling through the square. A thin squirrel stood on his haunches near an empty bench, eyeing Norm hopefully.

Shaking his head, the reporter held up his empty hands. "No peanuts today, mate."

The squirrel made a disdainful chittering noise before scurrying away to an oak tree.

Fallen leaves crunched underfoot as Norm hurried along the gravel path.

Patrolman McCrea was just passing the salon entrance when Norm arrived. "Morning, Mr. Levine."

"How're things up there? Any fresh corpses?"

Frowning, young McCrea said, "You shouldn't kid about death, sir."

"If I didn't, I'd be in even worse shape than I am now," the curly-haired reporter replied. "What I mean is, death is a very unsettling concept to live with. I'll be perfectly frank, it isn't something I'm especially anxious to try. Who needs oblivion, after all?"

"Don't you believe in the hereafter?"

"My lad, I'm not even one hundred percent sure about the here," admitted Norm. "I want to do a follow-up story on Reinman and the salon. May I pop up?"

"Sure, I'm just on my beat again. I'm not on guard here."

"Okay, then I'll ascend and put my fabled nose for news to work." He went up the steps two at a time.

The main room was empty and the door to Reinman's office was closed.

As Norm surveyed the place he thought he heard something from behind another of the doors. The noise made by something being banged against a hollow metal locker.

He decided to investigate. Once he opened the door he heard the sounds of a struggle coming from the far end of the corridor.

". . . your pet faggot ain't here now, Max. So you can't shove me around."

"I'm warning you, Ernie. I don't want you hanging around here no more."

"You know damn well I'm not hurting nothing."

Trotting to the open door of the locker room, Norm looked in. "Might an innocent passerby be of assistance?" he inquired, entering.

"Get the hell out of here," suggested Ernie Garcia, glowering at him.

The big fighter was standing, wide-legged, in the aisle between the rows of lockers. Max Reinman sat, his back against the door of a locker, on a bench.

"Levine, ain't you?" asked Reinman.

"The same, star reporter of the San Amaro *News-Hour.*" He bowed. "What seems to be the trouble, gents?"

"Listen, nobody wants any trouble," Garcia told him. "You just take a hike for yourself and—"

"It's you who got to get out, Ernie." When Reinman started to rise, the ex-boxer shoved him down.

"Tell you what," said Norm with an amiable smile as he started to back away. "I do believe I'll go place a call to the cops. They're eager to converse with you, Garcia."

"You're not calling nobody." Garcia came striding for him.

Norm saw the big right fist coming at him, but he just couldn't get out of the way in time.

Matt Prize found a forlorn Norm Levine in the offices of the San Amaro newspaper. It was a few minutes past noon and the reporter was sitting behind his desk in his cubbyhole of an office examining his face in a small rectangular mirror.

"Vanity, vanity," remarked Matt.

Lowering the mirror, Norm pointed at his chin. There was a bruise growing there. "Feast your eyes on that, old pal," he invited. "An enormous welt mars my otherwise classically macho puss."

Matt sat on the edge of his friend's desk. "Trouble at home?"

"Trouble at the Diana Aerobic Salon." He put the mirror, face down, on a clear patch of desk top. "In the person of Ernie Garcia."

"You found him?"

"He found me and his fist found my innocent chin," explained Norm. "I was as close to being out cold as you can come."

"What was Garcia doing there?"

"You mean in addition to decking harmless scribes? Apparently he was nosing around the locker rooms yet again," replied Norm. "Reinman discovered him and attempted to apply the proverbial bum's rush to his formidable person. I came traipsing in at that point and, like many a US military advisor overseas, ended up suffering violence myself."

"And Garcia took off?"

"Like a turkey through the corn. When I returned from the dead, he was long gone."

"The guy keeps going back there."

"Which is more than I intend to do." Norm glanced at the triptych frame that held photos of each of his wives to date. Shuddering, he turned that face down. "Once bopped, twice shy."

"Think you're capable of lunch?"

"As long as they don't mind my sipping it through a straw."

"I want to talk to Lofton. We might as well lunch at his restaurant at the same time."

"Lofton's Eden? Veggie food? You are asking a lad who just went one round with a heavyweight contender to suffer through a meatless meal?"

"They have, so I'm told, nice soup."

Norm said, "Okay. You want to depart now? I have an appointment to interview none other than Kevin Wagner, estranged hubby of the deceased, this very afternoon at exactly three at our posh yacht club. Care to tag along, by the way?"

"I have to be back on campus by four, but I would, yes," said Matt. "First off, though, I want to look through the paper's morgue and back issue file."

Spreading both arms wide, the reporter said, "Norman Levine, leading candidate for the Doormat of the Year Award, folks. His most intimate cronies walk all over him, use him shamelessly, and then reward him with nothing more than a handful of sunflower seeds."

"This should only take us a few minutes."

Norm got up. "If only somebody loved me for myself alone," he grumbled.

"Fascinating," commented Norm. "Fascinating." He was hunched over an open, bound volume of the *News-Hour*.

The two of them were in a musty room down beneath the newspaper offices. Metal shelves that rose from floor to ceiling held the bound, back issues of the daily paper, dating all the way to 1911. Along one wall were filing cabinets packed with folders of clippings and photos.

Matt, sitting two chairs over from his friend at the heavy wooden table, was examining the contents of a manila folder. "What the hell are you reading?"

"Did you know there was once a comic strip called 'Dan Dunn'? Yep, he was also known as Secret Operative #48 and the guy's a ringer for Dick Tracy. Here he is in full and glorious color," said Norm. "And what have we on the opposite page? 'Big Chief Wahoo' this one is entitled. The leading man seems to be a diminutive Indian fellow with a feathered headdress and an eccentric vocabulary. Ah, and get a gander at these paper dolls that accompany 'Jane Arden.' When not posing in her scanties for little scissor freaks, Jane was a girl reporter I gather. Do you think the ladies on the *News-Hour* wear lingerie like—"

"What year are you wading through?"

"1938."

"C'mon, I'm interested in three years ago, not ancient history."

"Yeah, but I've already read the funnies from the 1980s." Shrugging, he shut the volume, which caused dust and flecks of yellowing paper to flicker through the air. "Another of the hazards of the journalistic life is getting a hernia from toting these massive volumes around. Pity my tightwad employers have never heard of microfilm." He hefted the big book back to its place on the shadowy shelves. "What year are we interested in, did you say?"

"I want stuff on Ernie Garcia's arrest, on the gang he was a member of." Matt told him the year and the months he was concentrating on.

"Most of that would be in that folder you've got."

"Most, but it could be your clipper missed something."

"To hear is to obey, *tuan.*" He lifted a volume of newspapers from a nearer shelf. "This donkey work is good therapy. I've forgotten all about my sore chin."

"Good."

"Now I'm bothered exclusively by my aching back."

"Diamonds," said Matt, lifting out a clipping.

"That's what the missing loot was?"

"According to this account, the gang allegedly made off with five-hundred thousand in full-cut diamonds that were being shipped from the San Amaro Airport to a jewelry outfit back in Danbury, Connecticut."

"None of my wives looked good in diamonds, even the latest one." He opened the new volume. "That's why, though they never believe me, I didn't shower them with the things. So it was diamonds Garcia was involved with, I'd forgotten the details."

"The police found a Golden State Gem Associates bill of lading in the car Garcia was driving that night."

"Circumstantial."

"A security guard at the airport who was hit on the head during the snatch later identified Garcia."

Rubbing his chin, Norm said, "That part I can believe. They didn't find a single diamond on him, though, did they?"

"Nary a one. The assumption was Garcia hid them someplace before being caught."

"If he ever had them. Remember, he sure wasn't the brains of the mob."

"Nope, but he may've been carrying the loot. Or at least some of it." Matt returned the clipping to the folder. "None of the diamonds has ever surfaced, far as anyone knows. That indicates that somebody, possibly Garcia, stashed them."

Norm opened the volume of back-dated papers. "I recall a similar group of rascals operating in Chicago a few years ago," he said thoughtfully. "They were looting the airport and so on. Thing was, when the law finally caught them it turned out these lads were all businessmen types. White-collar execs who'd decided this was a nifty way to bolster their economy. Not one was a Mafia member or even had a previous criminal record. 'Course, that was Chicago.''

"Could be we had the same sort of thing here," said Matt. "And when the thing went sour, and Ernie was nabbed, they decided to fold up."

"Right. They could be a bunch of respected, sun-drenched citizens going about their business again as though nothing ever happened. Or, on the other hand, they could've been a band of the worst syndicate thugs around and they might have retired to Vegas where they're now peddling toot."

"If they happen to be local folks, though," said Matt, "they can't be too jolly inside."

"Not with five-hundred thousand dollars of ice still possibly sitting someplace unclaimed," said Norm. "Loot that my sparring partner, Ernie Garcia, may know the location of."

Nodding, Matt returned to going through the clipping file on the boxer.

After a few moments Norm said, "This is interesting."

"More funny papers?"

"No, an ad for Reinman's Gym. Says, 'We'll Reopen in One Week! All Water Damage Repaired! Lockers and Shower Room Now Better Than Ever !' " He tapped the half-page ad, sitting back. "I'd forgotten this, and I don't think any of the accounts mentioned it. But the gym was closed that whole fateful week, Matt. So on the night Garcia was netted, Reinman's wasn't even open. That could mean he hadn't been there at the gym that night at all."

"It could also mean," said Matt, "that was the reason he was there."

Chapter 11

NORM HAD BOTH ELBOWS RESTING ON THE table while he consulted the Lofton's Eden menu. "Amazing," he said, "how many different things can be stuffed into pita bread."

Matt was looking around the restaurant, which was only about half full. "Don't see anything of Stew Lofton," he said.

"I'm also astounded at the wide variety of objects that can be sprouted. Alfalfa, garbanzo beans, what—"

"Are you gentlemen ready to order?" asked the slim, dark-haired young woman who'd stopped alongside their table.

"As ready as I'll ever be." Norm shut his menu, assumed a stoic expression. "I'd like the barley-mushroom soup."

"Cup or crock?"

"Which is the lesser?"

"Cup."

"That's for me. Yum-yum."

"To drink?"

"Hemlock."

"Beg pardon?"

"Just water'll be fine."

"And you, sir . . . oh, you're Matthew Prize."

"I am," he admitted. "You must be Susan."

She smiled, lowering her order pad. "You're a friend of Jan Early's."

"Yep. I was hoping I could talk to Stew Lofton. Is he—"

"About last night, you mean? That was so terrible. Midge ate in here all the time."

"Is Lofton around?"

When she shook her head her long dark hair brushed at her shoulders. "He's at the doctor's again," she replied. "Because of his darned hand. Why those damn . . . well, I don't guess I better talk about that."

"You were here last night, too?"

"Sure." She sat in the third chair at the table. "You're a detective, aren't you?"

"Used to be. Now I'm just an interested citizen."

She said, "Midge was worried about something."

"Last night?"

"For the last few weeks at least. Sometimes she'd come in by herself and I'd sit with her long enough to have a cup of herb tea. So I got to know her some."

"What was she worried about?"

"I don't know for sure, but it had something to do with her husband, used-to-be husband."

"Kevin Wagner?"

"Midge never mentioned the man's name," she

answered. "She was divorced I know, or separated anyway. He wanted her to come back and lately he'd taken to phoning her a lot at her apartment. Pleading and threatening."

"What sort of threats?"

"Midge didn't spell it out," said Susan. "I'll tell you, though, I'm pretty sure from other conversations I had with her that this man hit her more than once while they were married and living together."

"One of America's favorite indoor sports," observed Norm, "wifebeating."

"Last night," said Matt, "did she mention anything specific? Any trouble, something that had just come up to upset her?"

"No, but she was a little more nervous than usual. Midge could always kid and be funny, but it was sort of strained last night."

"Did anything happen here? An argument with one of the women? Somebody at another table try to pick her up?"

"We don't serve booze," she answered with a small smile. "That cuts down on the squabbles and bird-dogging. There wasn't anything unusual last night, no."

"She left before the others?"

"Yes, she told me she had to get back to the salon. If she hadn't done that . . ."

"Anybody leave here the same time as Midge?"

Susan considered. "No, and I didn't notice anyone hanging around outside either."

"Maybe Lofton saw something," suggested Matt.

"I sort of doubt it. He had to go out before even Midge took off," Susan said. "To see our accountant. We have some kind of foul-up on our taxes."

"I'm looking for a good accountant," said Matt. "Who do you use?"

"Nathan Isenberg, over on Verdadero Street. I guess he's okay."

Norm said, "Matt, could you order before we continue? I find myself craving a cup of soup."

An incredibly beautiful red-haired young woman with an amazing tan and in a simple nine-hundred dollar frock was drifting out of the entrance of the yacht club bar, laughing back over her perfect left shoulder at someone still inside.

"Hold on to me, Matt," requested Norm in low tones as they approached the thick oaken door. "Don't let me turn into the dreaded wolfman and attack this stunning wench."

"I thought you only changed at night during a full moon."

"Lately it's been getting worse. I may need shots."

The lovely red-haired girl ignored them vigorously as she came striding along the plank walkway, heading for the edge of the fenced parking lot. "Miguelito?"

A wide-shouldered, handsome parking attendant in crimson jacket and tight black trousers came trotting over to her. "Your Jag, Miss du Plexus?"

"That's a jolly idea." She tossed him her keys.

"Onward," reminded Matt, reaching for the ornate brass doorknob.

"Sigh," said Norm, taking a final gaze across the gray afternoon at the beautiful redhead.

The door came flapping open again before Matt could touch it.

"Benny," called the tanned young man in blazer and flannels who came pushing out. "Who the hell are you trying to seduce now? Not that parking lot grease-ball?"

The girl paid him no mind.

"Not bad enough you play footsie with that jerk Reisberson all during lunch— Excuse me, sir." He'd staggered, bumped against Matt. "That bitch . . ."

"I guess maybe," said Norm, opening the door, "it's just as well Benny ignored us."

The bar and cocktail lounge occupied a large, L-shaped room and the walls facing the sea were of faintly tinted blue glass. The Pacific stretched away forever out beyond the beach and seemed to give off a pale blue glare.

A small bald man in a cocoa-colored suit hurried over to block their further progress. "Gentlemen, may I help you?"

"Why, sure," said Norm, digging his toe into the thick sea blue carpeting. "We're two hell-bent chicken farmers from up in Petaluma and we heard tell that this here place now is ideally suited for hell raising and general hoopdedoo. So we thought we'd drop in and lift us a few brews. Our only concern, though, is whether our six hundred fryers'll be safe parked out there in your dang lot."

The little man shuddered almost imperceptibly. "I fear, gentlemen, that only members may avail themselves of—"

"Actually, I'm Norm Levine of the San Amaro *News-Hour*," Norm told him. "We have an appointment with Kevin Wagner."

Relief came sighing out of him. "You're something of a tease, Mr. Levine, is that it?"

"I'm a rascal for sure. Is Wagner about?"

"At his usual table by the far window." He caught

the heavyset electronics heir's eye, nodded at Matt and Norm. Wagner's head ticked up and down once. "You may join him, gentlemen. I'll send a waiter over at once."

While they made their way across the room, Norm said, "I'm having second thoughts about the red-haired lady. You know, she might just be worth the grief."

Kevin Wagner said, "Very well, I'll drink alone then," and lifted his glass of scotch.

Out over the ocean a dozen or more gulls were circling, crying angrily, and then diving at the water.

"I never drink on duty," explained Norm. He had a steno book opened on the mosaic tile tabletop in front of him.

"Wouldn't a cassette recorder be better?" Wagner gestured at the open book.

"Gadgets make me uneasy."

Wagner chuckled. "Good thing I don't feel that way." He took another sip of his drink. "You say you don't work for the newspaper, Prize?"

"I'm just along as a sort of consultant," replied Matt. "If that bothers you I can—"

"Not at all, I never let little things annoy me." He turned to Norm. "I granted this interview, while turning down all those manicured, blow-dried oafs from Los Angeles and elsewhere, because you're with the local paper, Levine. There are a few things I want to say about Midge, but only to people who were, in a sense, her friends and neighbors."

The reporter asked, "How long were you married?"

Folding his large hands around the glass, Wagner watched the diving gulls. "All that fuss for some garbage," he observed. "Midge and I . . . her true name was Margaret, did you know?"

"Yep, I looked up her records."

"She and I were married for a little less than two years," continued Wagner. "I met her, of all places, at Wagner Electronics where she'd been working as a secretary. Despite what movies and television tell us, it's rather difficult to carry on a romance with a woman who works for you. At least it was for me, and she was, by the way, the very first Wagner employee I took a serious interest in. We were married for two years and then . . . there was an unfortunate misunderstanding. The marriage . . . seemed to fall apart after that. And Midge moved out on me."

Matt asked, "You parted friends?"

"Not the very best of friends," admitted Wagner. "Ah, I imagine you've heard rumors about my private life. That I beat women and—"

"We were only wondering," put in Norm, "if you kept in touch with her."

Wagner drank more of his drink. "Not really, no," he said. "That was her wish, not mine. Midge had long been interested in achieving a successful career in some area of show business. The job with Max Reinman was a step in that direction, though not, in my opinion, a wise one."

Matt shifted in his chair. "Did that embarrass you, your ex-wife working at an exercise salon?"

"Not especially, Mr. Prize, although I suppose I would've preferred she didn't."

"When's the last time you saw Midge Branner?" asked Norm.

"I still can't get used to the fact she was using her

maiden name," Wagner said. "I never saw her to speak to since she left me."

"But you have spoken to her over the phone," asked Matt, "haven't you?"

"What makes you suggest that, Prize?"

"Then you hadn't been telephoning her?"

"Even though our divorce became final some weeks ago," Wagner said, "I hadn't given up all hope. Yes, I did call my wife, my ex-wife, on a few occasions. To see if I couldn't persuade her to come back."

"You apparently weren't successful."

"I had the definite feeling she was giving the idea serious consideration, but then . . ." He shook his head sadly. "That's all unimportant now."

Norm asked, "You're paying for the funeral?"

"Midge had no close living relatives. There's a great-aunt back in Cambridge, Massachussets. She's seventy-seven, living on Social Security and couldn't care less about Midge. She doesn't intend to come to the funeral, even though I offered to fly her out and back."

"When's the funeral going to be?"

"Next Tuesday morning at ten. Saint Norbert's Church," answered Wagner. "And there'll be a memorial service Monday evening at eight at the Johnson Brothers Funeral Home."

Matt said, "When you talked to Midge Branner over the phone, did she mention any trouble or problems she was having?"

"She wasn't one to confide, even when we were married." He drank a sip of scotch. "But I know of no one who'd threatened her or had any reason to do her violence."

"You yourself," asked Matt, "never threatened her?"

Wagner set his glass on the table. "Mr. Levine," he said slowly and carefully, "I'll be happy to answer any of *your* questions, but I believe I've had just about enough of your friend's third degree."

Norm made his eyes go wide. "It certainly wasn't our intention to upset you," he said. "You mentioned having some sort of statement to make?"

"Yes, I want it known that I am offering a reward of five-thousand dollars to anyone who provides information leading to the arrest of my wife's murderer." He sat back in his chair. "I have nothing further to say. Good afternoon."

Norm shut his notebook and he and Matt left the table. As they headed for the way out, he asked Matt, "You had, I presume, a reason for needling him?"

"I was curious," replied Matt, "as to how violent he might get when you make him angry."

Chapter 12

PUFFING SOME AND LEAVING A FAINT TRAIL of sand, Matt entered the house by way of the kitchen door. It was a few minutes before nine on a warm, clear Saturday morning. Gulls were calling plaintively out over the calm sea.

"How many miles?" asked Jan. She was at the stove boiling water for tea, wearing new yellow warm-up pants he hadn't seen before.

Leaning against the wall, he held up two fingers.

"You're wheezing like a circus calliope," she observed. "And do you know why? It's because you've got chocolate-coated lungs. All that candy and other junk food you gobble—"

"When's the last time you heard a circus calliope?" He straddled a chair.

"Let's see? It was at Circus World in Florida, fall of 1981."

"Well, actually I'm more melodious than one of those."

Jan poured boiling water into her teacup. "Lieutenant Redding called while you were out callioping around."

"Something important?"

"He wants you to phone him, but he didn't seem especially anxious or excited."

Matt left the chair. "I wish you hadn't tossed my Cocoa Puffs out. I'm in the mood for a heaping bowl of—"

"Ugh," she remarked.

At the wall phone he dialed the police station and asked for Redding. "Lieutenant? Matt Prize."

"What's the matter with you? You have a chest cold?"

"Been running."

"I'm glad I'm not in shape to try that," said the policeman. "I have a few items for you. The blood on those abandoned warm-up pants is group 0. Same as Midge Branner's."

Matt nodded. "Been able to trace the pants themselves?"

"Not yet, and I'm not sure we ever will," answered Lieutenant Redding. "It's now absolutely certain the woman wasn't sexually molested in any way. We've talked to all but two of the ladies enrolled in the dancing classes at Reinman's joint. Not one admits having dropped in there on Thursday night. To be on the safe side, I'm checking alibis. The two ladies I haven't interviewed are both out of town. One on business in Chicago, one on vacation to Vermont."

"What about Ernie Garcia? I understand he's been seen at the salon again."

"We located him. Back at his apartment yesterday afternoon," said the lieutenant. "We invited him in and had a long chat."

"You holding him?"

"No."

"Where's he been?"

"Ernie says he got sick Thursday night, food poisoning, and passed out in an alley behind a Chinese restaurant down on Del Rio Drive. He spent Friday in the park, too sick to work."

"You buying any of that?"

"We're checking it all out. We know he did actually have dinner at the Golden Mandarin at about nine on Thursday."

"Was he at the salon that night?"

"Ernie claims no."

Matt watched as Jan took her cup of peppermint tea over to the kitchen table and sat. "Lieutenant, I'm curious about that robbery at the airport. The one Ernie was involved in."

"Yeah?"

"Do you have anything that wasn't in the papers at the time?"

"Not much."

"But the diamonds never showed up?"

"They didn't, no," Redding said. "My guess is that Ernie knows something about that."

"The rest of the gang, could they have been white-collar types and not pro criminals?"

"They could've been little green weirdos from Mars for all we ever found out," answered the lieutenant. "Ernie simply never talked. Do you have something on who did the job?"

"Nothing, just curious. I remember a rumor at the

time that a cop or detective might have been involved."

"The press loves rumors like that. Say, I hear you chatted with Kevin Wagner yesterday."

"Yep, during the cocktail hour."

"That could be anytime around the clock with that guy."

"He's offering a reward for the killer."

"Yeah, I know. We've already had two psychics and a nitwit call in with helpful suggestions," said Redding. "Have you come up with anything else on your own?"

"Nothing concrete," said Matt. "Call you if I do. So long."

The San Amaro Campus of Cal State covered fifteen rolling acres overlooking the Pacific Ocean. Although many of the adobe, wrought-iron, and red tile buildings looked as though they dated back to California's mission days, there wasn't a structure older than ten years. There were grassy lawns, and cypresses and palms lining the roads and walkways.

At a few minutes after one in the afternoon that Saturday, Matt and Jan were walking along one of the curving lanes toward Kramer Hall, where Matt's office was. A faint sea wind touched them as they crossed a rustic bridge over a snaking creek.

"I'm feeling especially ancient today," confessed Jan. "Hard to believe it's already six long years since I graduated from these hallowed halls."

"I'll stick by you, no matter how old and feeble you grow," he pledged. "Up to age thirty, that is. Then I trade you in."

She took hold of his arm. "I'm trying not to think

about Midge," she said. "I know I should go to that memorial service on Monday night, but . . . will the coffin be closed?"

"Yes."

"Then I won't have to look at her body. Maybe that won't make it so bad."

"I'll be with you."

"You don't have to go just to—"

"I want to see who shows up."

"Then you're still working on this?"

"In an unofficial way."

"You miss the private investigating, don't you?"

"Sometimes," he admitted. They reached the crest of the hill and there was the three-story brick and red tile building that housed the Law and Criminology Departments. "But being an amateur now, that means I can pick and choose. I really got tired of skip tracing and deadbeat hounding. Didn't like a lot of the industrial spying cases either. And after the fourth or fifth case where you're hired to track down a goofy parent who's kidnapped the kids from the ex-spouse . . . Compared to all that, the academic life is a bed of roses."

"You'll go back to doing it someday."

"Maybe." They went up the steps, side by side.

"What do you think about Midge's murder? You haven't talked about it much with me."

"I'm not sure yet why she was killed." He held the glass door open for her. "There are several possibilities."

"I've been thinking about the person whom the patrolman and Rod Flanders noticed," she said. "They both said it was a woman, but it doesn't have to be. Anybody could dress up in a warm-up suit."

Matt said, "That's one of the possibilities I've been kicking around, Jan."

"A man who dressed up like a woman, though, he'd be a pretty strange sort of person. Which comes back to my original notion that it was a madman. That her murder was a sex crime."

"Don't think it was a sex crime, not in the strictest sense anyway."

"Why do you give me the impression you're being evasive?"

"Because you're a fair detective yourself, and I am being evasive."

"Meaning you don't want to share your thoughts?"

"Not yet."

The office of the Criminology Department was at the rear of the first floor. The door was unlocked, but no one was inside. Matt went on in with Jan in tow. He went behind the reception counter and got his mail out of the nest of cubbyholes on the wall.

"Look at Professor Dana's hole. He always gets three times as much mail as I do."

"He's the grand old man of the department," she reminded him.

Matt waited until they were again out in the afternoon sunlight to sort through the handful of mail he'd gotten since yesterday. "Scholars Discount Book Sale . . . Benevolent Order of Ex-Chiefs of Police Annual Oktoberfest . . . one of my old students who's now a private investigator in Detroit . . . This is interesting."

"What?"

He was holding a postal card out from the batch, looking from the message side to the address side. "Wasn't even postmarked. Somebody just slipped it into my box."

Jan took the card from his hand and read the block-lettered message aloud. " 'Stick to your books, professor! Forget about Midge!' "

"Looks like somebody's trying to scare me off," he said.

Jan handed the card back to him. "They don't know you very well then."

Chapter 13

"YOU'D BETTER GET OUT OF THERE," warned Betsy Grossman.

"Can't hear you," called Rick Grossman from the next room.

"We're going to be late." She was sitting at her dressing table, adjusting the dark wig she planned to wear this evening.

Wrapped in a fluffy hotel towel, a souvenir of their last trip to the Caribbean, her husband came hurrying into the master bedroom. "What the hell time is it?"

"Seven-fifteen."

"You kidding me? Why didn't you tell me earlier that—"

"I did. The sitter's already here, down with the kids in the family room. You had the shower running and you were making that godawful mooing that you claim is singing, so you didn't hear me."

"I have a great voice." He was a middle-size man in his early thirties, nearly ten pounds overweight. "Why do you keep hiding my underwear?"

"You'll find it in the same place as always."

"Here it is, in the wrong drawer."

Betsy turned to watch him. "You don't really want to go, do you?"

"Sure, I do. What makes you think I don't?"

"You're dragging your feet like a kid on the first day of school."

"Not so, Betsy. I mean, why wouldn't I be looking forward to going to a wake." He'd put on fresh underwear and was now hopping as he tugged on a sock. "After the sort of a day I've had over at Wagner Electronics, a nice memorial service'll cheer me up."

"Is he insisting you attend?"

"He? Do you mean the deity himself, Kevin Wagner."

"Is he, Rick?"

"Not directly, no." Hurrying to a closet, he grabbed out a white shirt. "Wagner just issued one of his typical memos to the junior and senior executive staff. 'I don't want any of you to feel you're obliged to attend the memorial service for my late wife at the Johnson Brothers Funeral Home this evening at eight P.M.' Hell, even a junior exec like me can read between those lines."

"You aren't really happy there, are you?"

"Sure, I am. I'm deliriously happy." He was climbing into the trousers of his most somber gray suit. "Today they had to warn me more than once to quit laughing and chuckling so much."

"You could get another job at any—"

"Sure, and while I'm looking for a new job the

bank'll forget about the one thousand six hundred fifty dollars that's due on our mortgage each and every month. The orthodontist will allow us to postpone the three hundred ten dollars per month we—"

"Rick, we have a savings account, plus savings certificates. We've enough money to—"

"Enough to last us maybe two months." He leaned toward her mirror to knot his dark tie.

Betsy reached up, touched his fresh-shaved cheek. "This is the only life we've got. There's no reason to be miserable or—"

"I'm not exactly miserable, Betsy. Wagner pays well, which makes his tyrannies easier to put up with. And fortunately he doesn't even come in every day." Rick plucked his suit coat up off the bed and shrugged into it.

His wife said, "I wonder why he's making such a show of mourning Midge."

"Guilty conscience."

"About what?" She stood up.

"The lousy way he treated the lady when she was alive." He made a final inspection of himself in the mirror. "I remember, back when they were married, her coming around to W.E. Even makeup couldn't always hide the damage."

"He was beating her?"

Rick shrugged. "Somebody was." He took his wife's arm. "Okay, let's go pay our respects to the dead."

"Ah, but you are," Kevin Wagner informed his sister.

"No, I can't. I'm ill." She was slumped in an armchair in their large beam-ceilinged living room, toying absently with the diamond bracelet on her wrist.

"You aren't sick at all, Sis." He was standing with his back to the dead fireplace. He loomed immense in his tight-fitting black suit.

"I am. I'm having terrible stomach cramps, and chills," she said in a blurred pleading voice. "There's a new flu bug going—"

"The only thing affecting you is booze. Now get your act together and—"

"I don't drink any longer, Kevin. It's awful of you to keep insinuating that—"

"C'mon, dear heart. You smell like the rag used to mop up a skid-row bar."

Lizbeth began to cry softly. "I won't go," she insisted. "Neither should you. You hounded the poor girl when she was alive, leave her in peace now she's dead."

"Midge was my wife."

"No, she wasn't. You were legally divorced."

He crossed the big room, slowly, and stopped in front of her chair. "Sometimes I think you hated her more than I did. Come on, we'll be late for the memorial service if we don't leave at once."

"You'll really have to go without me then. I'm much too ill to—"

"I've had enough of this crap, Sis." He grabbed her arm, yanked her to her feet. "So please don't annoy me any further." He slapped her twice, hard, across the face.

Lizbeth whimpered, fell back into the chair. "You're a toad," she muttered. "A miserable, evil toad."

"Be that as it may, you'll do what I say." He pulled her to her feet again.

A misty rain was falling.

Curt Sloane slowed their car going around a twisting downhill bend in the night road. "Perfect night to go to a memorial service," he remarked.

"The service won't last that long," said Connie, toying with the pair of gloves on her lap.

"Ten minutes of this sort of stuff is too much for me."

"I know, but it's something I have to do."

He watched the windshield wipers tick back and forth. "Why?"

"I explained all that, Curt. Midge Branner was my instructor and, starting to be anyway, my friend."

"You only had three sessions at that idiotic salon and you're not even enrolled there any longer. So there's really—"

"I don't see why you made me quit. They're going to begin the class again next week with Rod Flanders filling in until—"

"There was a murder there, Con. A brutal sex crime," her husband reminded her. "The place simply isn't safe. Reinman agrees with me. He gave us a refund, which—"

"I'd have liked to go on. After all, it was your idea in the first place for me to go to—"

"That was my mistake. I didn't realize what a dump the salon was, never having seen the setup, when you enrolled. If I had—"

"Is it the money, Curt? I mean, I know you said we can afford it, but if you think it's too much of a strain on our budget, I think I can borrow some from my sister and—"

"Sure, that'd be great. She thinks little enough of me already."

"Arlene likes you. If you'd make a little effort to—"

"We are not on the skids. We are not in deep financial trouble," he said evenly as he concentrated on the rainy road.

"I didn't mean that. And as soon as Mrs. Mott takes the Berrill place, why, the commission on that—"

"The old bitch changed her mind. She's now thinking about a condo in Pacific Palisades."

"I'm sorry," said his wife.

"Nothing to be sorry about. We're a long way from going under," he said. "And things are starting to look better in the whole real estate market hereabouts."

"If only I could help."

He reached over and patted her hand. "You do help, Con," he said. "Just don't fret so much."

Matt parked his car in the lot at the side of the Johnson Brothers Funeral Home. "Here we are."

The building was two stories high, designed to look somewhat like a rustic English chapel. The pink, gold, and blue spotlights planted in the ground illuminated the walls and detracted some from the effect.

After turning off the motor and setting the brake, Matt reached across Jan's lap to open the glove compartment. "We'll go on in a minute."

"Not too many mourners here ahead of us."

"Yep, I wanted to be here early." He was groping in the cubicle. "To see the visitors as they arrive and sign in."

"Are you searching for something?" she inquired innocently.

"My spare stash of Nestlé's Crunch bars. I had six or seven of them stored here for . . . Ah, I see it all. *Had* is the correct tense, since I no longer *have* them."

"Well, I did clean out your car yesterday," admitted Jan. "You had an incredible amount of garbage stuffed in the glove compartment, Matt. Old insurance cards, road maps of places like Iowa and Nebraska, garage receipts, old parking tickets."

"Don't tell me you tossed out my collection of parking tickets, too?"

"I stored everything in a shoe box in the garage."

"Including the candy?"

Jan thought about it. "I may have dropped that in the garbage, by mistake."

Muttering, he climbed free of his car. "I'm going to need a lot of energy tonight," he said as the rain started hitting down on his tan raincoat. The wind brought the briny smell of the sea. "And it is a sound medical fact that chocolate and sugar provide an—"

"That's a lot of bunk." She let herself out, joined him on the slick asphalt of the lot. "All chocolate does is futz up your system. And with a system like yours, Matthew, you really can't afford another screw-up."

He started striding toward the side door of the funeral parlor. "Don't drink, don't smoke, hardly even fool around with other women," Matt said. "Chocolate candy is my only known vice and then you deprive me of—"

"Hush up now." Jan reached for the door handle.

They entered a quiet hallway, its walls were pale

pink and the thick carpeting a salmon color. The smells of flowers and disinfectant mixed in the warm air. Somewhere organ music murmured mournfully.

"You don't think Midge's killer will show up here tonight?" she asked him.

"I'm counting on it," he said.

Chapter 14

NORM LEVINE HUNCHED HIS SHOULDERS AND shivered once. "Remind me not to die," he said in a low voice. "I couldn't put up with all this."

He and Matt were standing at the rear of the reception room in the suite where Midge Branner's body was laid out. The coffin itself was in a smaller room beyond, surrounded by wreaths and flowers. The visitors were filing in now and the routine, overseen by one of the solemn-faced Johnson Brothers, was to sign the leatherbound visitors' book that rested on an ornate little table near the entryway, pass by the closed casket in the next room, and then take a seat in the reception room.

Matt seemed particularly interested in the signing-in process.

Norm inquired. "Thinking of going into autograph collecting?"

"Max Reinman is right-handed," said Matt. "Rod Flanders is, too."

"So is yours truly. So?"

"And here comes the stricken widower."

Kevin Wagner, firmly guiding his pale sister, had entered. He paused just over the threshold to scan the room.

Three of the men in the room stiffened slightly.

"Wagner Electronics employees I'll wager," said Norm.

When Wagner let go of his sister to sign the guest book, she swayed and had to catch hold of the back of an empty chair.

He frowned, muttered something, and signed the book with his left hand.

"A southpaw," observed Norm. "Does that prove anything, Herr Professor?"

"Just might."

The Sloanes arrived next and Curt signed the book.

"Another right-hander," said Norm. "This is getting to be fun. Want to bet on what the next one'll be?"

Rick Grossman signed for himself and his wife. He was left-handed.

"Glad we decided not to bet," said the reporter. "The odds favored a right-hander."

Lieutenant Redding entered, glanced around, and came over to them. "Haven't heard from you in a day or so, Matt."

"Nothing to report."

"Same here," admitted the policeman. He reached for his cigarettes, remembered where he was, and stopped.

Stew Lofton and Susan got there next. They hesitated over the guest book and then the dark haired young woman signed for herself and the injured restaurant owner.

"Speaking of hands," said Norm, "have you considered what a nice alibi a bandaged hand makes?"

"The injury's real," said Matt.

Redding said, "Yeah, we checked with his doctor. A serious burn."

"Just a thought," said Norm. "My notions of criminology derive chiefly from something like forty-six Agatha Christie novels I read while in college. That taught me always to go for the least likely suspect."

"We've got a whole damn room full of unlikely suspects," grumbled Lieutenant Redding.

A plump middle-aged man, bearded and black-suited, entered the room. He went up to the attending Johnson Brother. "Here I am," he announced.

"Ah, good evening, Father Busino."

"I'd like to have a few words with . . . Mr. Wagner, is it?"

"The bereaved husband, yes. He's back in the family room, father."

Nodding, the priest started for the coffin.

He hadn't reached Kevin Wagner when Ernie Garcia came barging in. "Evening, everybody," the drunken boxer said loudly.

"Trouble," said Norm, brightening.

"Just want to tell you all something," said Garcia, chuckling. "Whoever's been looking can quit. I've got the stuff back and it's going to stay mine. So you—"

"Please, sir. I must insist you keep quiet." The funeral director reached a hand toward the ex-boxer.

"I said all I come to say. Just a little friendly

warning." He slapped the man's hand aside, spun, and went running out of there.

"Want to talk to him." Matt hurried to the doorway.

Out in the corridor he saw a side door easing closed. He stepped through it and out into the rainy night.

"Sucker." Garcia had been waiting in the shadows by the graveled path.

He hit Matt once in the stomach. Then, as Matt doubled up, Garcia delivered two sharp blows to his chin.

Matt dropped to his knees. The rain came slamming down at him. He tried to get up, to take a swing at the boxer. Instead he tumbled over into a neatly clipped hedge.

He was sitting in his car, in the passenger seat. The car was still parked in the funeral home lot. The rain drummed loudly on the roof. "No, I'm okay," Matt was saying.

Jan sat behind the wheel. "Nevertheless, I'm going to take you to the emergency room and have—"

"The guy only knocked me down, Jan. Nothing's broken. Really."

"Well, Lieutenant Redding agrees you ought to be looked at by a doctor."

Matt remembered being picked up and helped over to the car by Redding and Norm. "It's embarrassing," he said. "To have people think an old broken-down fighter, a palooka they used to call 'em, that he could deck me."

"Forget your pride. We have to get you—"

"The only reason Garcia was able to punch me at all," said Matt as he brushed at his damp and muddy suit, "was because he ambushed me. He was waiting out there to sock the first idiot who came after him. Smart. Then he could get away in the confusion which—"

"You sound a little dippy. Please, let's drive to the—"

"Nope, home'll be sufficient. A cup of cocoa and bed'll fix me up fine."

"Sure, chocolate is just what you need to—"

"Home."

She gave a resigned sigh and started the car. "Did you learn anything tonight?"

"Quite a bit."

"What exactly was Ernie Garcia babbling about?"

"It might've been a bluff." Matt leaned back in his seat as Jan headed the car homeward. "Or he may've been telling the truth."

"What is it he claims to have then?"

"The loot from that airport job."

"A fortune in diamonds?"

"More than likely."

She concentrated on her driving for a moment. "That doesn't seem quite right to me," she said finally. "What I mean is, Matt, if I had hundreds of thousands of dollars in stolen gems, I don't believe I'd brag about it in public."

"You're not a drunken boxer. Ernie Garcia's not as bright as you."

"Even so, I wouldn't have thought he was dumb enough to blurt that out in front of Lieutenant Redding."

"He probably didn't expect the lieutenant to be at the wake," Matt said. "Garcia was interested in delivering his message to someone else who was there tonight."

"Who?"

"His former partner," answered Matt.

Chapter 15

THE RAIN DIDN'T BOTHER HIM. HE STOOD IN the alley, patiently, while the hard night rain hit at him. Eyes narrowed, Ernie Garcia watched the sidewalk across the way.

"Coast is clear now," he murmured.

The husky boxer left the mouth of the alley, went running across the rain-swept street.

Garcia made it safely to the vacant lot. Crouched low, he worked his way through the weeds and high grass. He stepped on a broken wine bottle, nearly tripped and fell on the muddy ground. But he kept going.

When he reached the far edge of the lot, he crouched behind the board fence. He listened, heard nothing but water gurgling down through drain pipes and rain hitting the metal lids of the garbage cans lined up behind the old pink stucco apartment house.

"Stupid bastards," he said to himself, pushing at the loose board in the fence.

They never ever bothered to put a cop back here. So it was easy to sneak in and out of his place.

Pushing through the weak spot in the fence, Garcia sloshed across the backyard and over to the cellar door.

The door couldn't lock anymore, Garcia'd seen to that. He let himself in, waited inside the door while his eyes got used to the dimness.

It smelled of damp earth down here. Damp earth, old clothes, musty suitcases, piles of old newspapers, heating oil, and rats.

He crossed the room, climbed the short flight of wooden steps to the door, and stopped to listen again.

He could hear the landlady's television going in her ground-floor apartment. A lot of gunfire and tire squeals were coming out of the set.

Easing the door open, he entered the downstairs hall. There was an overturned tricycle sprawled on the threadbare carpet. Garcia skirted that and went on up the stairs. He knew which of the steps creaked and was able to sneak up to his second-floor apartment without making a sound.

This was going to be his last visit to this dump. He'd get the stuff from where he'd hidden it, grab the suitcase he'd already packed, and get the hell out of here.

He fumbled out his keys and got the green-painted door open.

Probably he should've taken off earlier, soon as he'd found the damn stuff. But he'd wanted to go to the funeral parlor tonight, anxious to make his little speech and let somebody know what the real situation was.

Chuckling, Garcia reached for the light switch. Then he realized the lights were already on.

He knew damn well he hadn't left them on.

He shut the door by leaning back against it and then scanned the room.

"Christ!"

Somebody'd been here, gone through the place. The drawers had been pulled out of the bureau. The cushion was off his armchair, the sheets and blankets had been stripped from his bed. Even the suitcase he'd carefully packed earlier was lying open, its contents scattered on the floor.

Taking it all in, slowly, Garcia began to get worried.

"Shouldn't have gone there tonight," he said aloud. "Should've kept quiet."

Nodding his head, he shuffled into the bathroom.

"Yeah, but nobody'd think to look here."

The chipped procelain lid to the toilet's water tank didn't appear to be disturbed.

Garcia, carefully, lifted the lid off. Rolling up his coat and shirt sleeves, he dived his right hand into the chill water.

Then he heard the shower curtain flutter behind him.

Before he could turn around an arm went around his neck.

Norm Levine made another slow circuit of Matt's chair. "No, he looks okay to me, Jan."

"You're no doctor," she pointed out from the living-room sofa. "To me he still looks sort of dazed and—"

"Whoa," suggested Matt. "I'm commencing to feel like I ought to be spread out on a morgue table, the way you ghouls are talking about me."

"He always looks a little dazed," added Norm while settling into an armchair. "You just haven't noticed it until now."

"Right," said Matt, "it's simple chocolate addict's stupor."

Jan spread her hands wide. "Okay, I'll quit harping on the state of your health."

"Did I miss much at the memorial service?" he asked the reporter.

"The festivities went without a hitch after you left," answered Norm. "Ernie Garcia's entrance proved to be the high spot of the evening. Gave me a nice bit to use in my article for *mañana*'s paper, too."

"Nobody else had anything to announce?"

"Father Busino gave a nice little speech, hampered only by the fact that he had no idea who Midge Branner was," the reporter said. "Kevin Wagner sobbed. Various Wagner Electronics toadies at the gathering radiated both sympathy and fear of job loss. All in all, old fellow, a typical fun-filled evening amidst the elite of this affluent little pocket of Southern California culture."

"Everything ties together somehow," said Matt. "Midge's murder, Ernie Garcia, the business tonight."

"Which means the unsolved airport robbery is linked in, too."

Nodding, Matt said, "Sure, that's probably—"

The phone rang.

"Sit," ordered Jan. "I'll get it." She hurried to the nearest phone, which was in the kitchen.

Norm leaned forward. "You do look a tad woozy,"

he said. "Are you sure you don't maybe have a mild concussion or—"

"Don't you start. I'm tip-top and—"

"Matt," called Jan. "It's Lieutenant Redding."

He heaved himself up out of the chair. "Be right there." Matt walked into the kitchen and took the receiver from Jan. "Hello, lieutenant."

"How are you feeling?"

"Not bad. Thoughtful of you to—"

"Are you well enough to come out?"

"Guess so. Where to?"

"Ernie Garcia's apartment," said the policeman. "Somebody's killed him."

Matt asked, "How?"

"Just about the exact same way the Branner woman was killed. A messy job with a knife."

"See you in fifteen minutes," promised Matt and hung up.

Chapter 16

LIEUTENANT REDDING LIT A CIGARETTE. "He was killed about ten tonight," he said, exhaling smoke.

He and Matt were standing beside Ernie Garcia's disordered bed. The boxer's body lay half in and half out of the bathroom, face down and wreathed with blood stains.

There were half a dozen other policemen in the small apartment: taking pictures, dusting for fingerprints, poking around.

Norm Levine was out in the hallway, along with a couple other reporters, trying to get a coherent story out of Garcia's tipsy landlady.

Matt looked away from the body toward a rain-spattered window. "Garcia wasn't kidding tonight at the memorial service."

"He really must've had something." Redding was

staring absently down at the dead man. "Or at least he convinced somebody he did."

Matt glanced around the room. "The killer searched this place and probably found it." He nodded toward the bathroom. "The lid's off the water tank, a pretty good indication that Garcia had something hidden there."

"Or that the killer thought he did."

"But the apartment was searched before Garcia came home tonight." Matt pointed at the body. "He's lying on top of some of the clothes that'd been tumbled out of his bureau. That stuff was dumped before he was killed, not after. He was trying to get clear of the bathroom when he was stabbed, so you have to figure he went in there. Now a guy who comes home and finds his place ransacked probably doesn't go right into the john just to relieve himself. He went to check on the stuff he had hidden."

"And the killer, who was hiding in the shower stall, jumped him and took off," said Redding, puffing on his cigarette. "There are traces of mud in the stall. And the landlady, for what her word's worth, swears she heard somebody fall and somebody else running out of here."

"Right, there was no time to look for it after the killing."

"This 'it' is what we've both been talking about," said the lieutenant. "You figure it was diamonds."

"I'd bet on it, yeah." He turned his back on the body. "Garcia made the mistake of bragging tonight. He was drunk, feeling cocky. So he crashed the wake."

"And somebody who was there tonight knew that Ernie was speaking the gospel truth." Redding took a slow drag on the cigarette, then coughed. "They figured he'd picked up the loot from wherever it'd been stashed and had it here in his apartment now."

"Could be the killer had searched this room before, back when Garcia first got out. The diamonds weren't here then." Matt kicked at the open suitcase. "Looks like Garcia was planning to take off. But he couldn't resist taunting his ex-partner before doing that."

"Not smart of him."

"Garcia wasn't brilliant, and booze seems to have inspired him to take extra risks," said Matt. "Still he was clever enough to get hold of those diamonds in the first place and hide them safely before he got picked up."

"He more than likely hid them at Reinman's Gym," said Redding. "That's why he's been hanging around there. Waiting for a chance to retrieve them."

Nodding, Matt said, "Garcia hadn't counted on the gym turning into a ladies-only salon while he was away. That made things a lot tougher."

Redding shoved his hands into his trouser pockets and gazed up at the peach-colored ceiling for a moment. "Hell, Matt, there were about seventy-five people at the funeral parlor tonight," he said unhappily. "And almost all of them were there when Garcia made his entrance. Any one of them could've slipped over here to search his apartment and kill Garcia when he stumbled in."

Redding contemplated that for a few silent seconds. "Judging from the wounds, Ernie Garcia and Midge Branner were more than likely killed by the same person. And it probably took a man to overpower and stab and an ex-boxer like Ernie."

"Not necessarily," Matt replied. "He was drunk

when we saw him earlier. In his condition, an athletic woman might have done it. And with all that exercising, none of the women in this case is a weakling."

"Yeah," said the policeman.

Norm scrutinized the all-night restaurant once more before settling into the booth. "I don't think this is the best place in the universe to order chocolate pie, old buddy," he warned Matt.

Grinning, Matt said, "Trust me. I've been here before."

"To Casanova's Sea Shanty? Why?"

"Back when I was a private investigator and worked a lot at night I discovered it," replied Matt. "The food is pretty good."

Jerking a thumb toward the low, green ceiling, Norm pointed out, "They still use fly paper. They've got spools of it dangling from the rafters, thick with defunct flies. Remind me not to order the rice pudding."

Matt tried his coffee. "What'd Garcia's landlady have to say?"

"Do you know what her name is?"

"Nope."

"Lovie McRobb." He yawned, then laughed. "Even in my wildest college days I never encountered a lady with a name like that. I drew the line at Corky Sankowitz."

"I remember Corky. Tall girl."

"Six feet one isn't tall. Not these days."

"You were talking about what Mrs. McRobb had to impart," nudged Matt.

Yawning, Norm shook his head as though he had water in his ears. "Forgive me, old saddle pard, I get groggy every night about this time," he said. "Anyway, she says she heard a thud from above, followed by the pitter-patter of running feet. She roused herself from her evening's video fare and climbed up to Garcia's ménage to tell him to cease dropping heavy stuff on the floor."

"Why'd she pick Garcia's apartment?"

"His palatial digs are right above hers," answered the reporter. "She knew right off where the noise was originating."

"She hadn't heard anything earlier, when the killer was up there alone, rummaging around?"

"The old dear is half crocked and had the telly on loud. It took somebody dropping dead overhead to get her attention."

"And she didn't see anyone?"

"Only her deceased tenant. The runner was gone."

"Had Garcia lived in that apartment house before?"

"No, only since he emerged from the slammer."

"Anything suspicious happen while he's been living there?"

"Matt, people who rent apartments from Mrs. McRobb are always up to something shady and suspicious. That's the sort of dump it is," Norm reminded him. "As far as Garcia is concerned, she thinks he came and went a lot at odd hours, but he didn't bother anyone."

"He hadn't given notice, had he?"

"She didn't mention it. Was he planning to skip?"

"He packed a suitcase."

"Then he . . ." Norm paused when the plump, sleepy-eyed waitress brought over a wedge of chocolate pie and placed it in front of his friend. "That looks more navy blue in color than chocolate brown."

"It's the last piece," she explained before going away.

Matt picked up the fork that had come with it. "Mrs. McRobb hadn't seen any unusual hangers-around?"

"All her clientele looks odd and unusual," Norm said. "She maintains, however, that she wasn't aware of anyone lurking around tonight. She's never had a murder there before, by the way. That'd make a nice slogan. 'McRobb Apartments. Eleven Years in Business and Only One Murder So Far!' "

Matt ate a bite of his pie. "What about—"

"How is it?"

"Hmm?"

"The pie."

"Fine, as I expected. Now, what about visitors to Garcia? Legitimate ones, regulars."

"Mrs. McRobb never knew him to have a caller, not even a lady friend."

"Damn it, he knew who killed Midge Branner," said Matt. "If I'd been able to talk to the guy tonight I—"

"Hey, he knocked you out."

"Even so."

"You sure as hell tried to talk to the bastard."

"That wasn't good enough," said Matt.

Chapter 17

RICK GROSSMAN PACED THE MASTER BEDroom. He had on his trousers, socks, and button-down blue shirt. No shoes as yet, no suit coat, and his tie wasn't tied. "The hell with it," he said.

Betsy, wearing a pale blue robe, was sitting on the edge of the unmade king-size bed. "You're certain you want to do this?"

Her husband crossed to the windows. The morning was gray; a fuzzy rain was falling down on their half acre of front lawn. "I've made up my mind," he said positively. "I went to that damn silly memorial service last night, but I am not going to the funeral. The hell with it."

"Maybe you ought to just stay home. The stress of the past few—"

"No, Betsy, I'm going in to Wagner Electronics. I will sit at my desk and do an honest day's work," he told her. "But I'm not driving out to the Holy Rest Cemetery to see them plant Wagner's former wife in the ground."

"Rick, Midge was a nice—"

"I've got nothing against her. Hell, I hardly knew the lady. What I'm bitching about is the way Wagner tells us what we're supposed to do every damn minute. I mean, he hired me to work at W.E. He didn't buy me."

"Do whatever you think is best," his wife said. "I've already told you I think you can get a better job almost—"

"Oh, I'm not quitting. No, not at all." He faced his wife. "I'm simply not going to be treated like a circus pony anymore. Let the bastard fire me and then let him try to explain it was because I didn't happen to attend his wife's funeral. I'll sue his pants off. Hell, she isn't even his wife any longer." He shook his head. "Last night really did it. Seeing him cry those crocodile tears . . . and that sister of his falling-down drunk."

"Lizbeth's not a bad person. She has the flu and—"

"Sure, the Russian Flu. From too many vodka martinis."

"Don't you think, Rick, considering the mood you're in, it would be better to stay home to—"

"Aren't you supporting me at all?" He took a couple of steps in her direction.

"Of course I am. I've thought Kevin Wagner was an ogre ever since you—"

"Okay, then support me. I'm going to the office."

Betsy left the bed. "Want some orange juice or—"

"I'm not much in the mood for breakfast."

"You ought to have something. This is going to be a rough day."

139

"An English muffin then. That's all."

Passing him, she touched his arm. "I do believe in you," she said quietly.

"I know, I know." He moved to the mirror to tie his tie.

Kevin Wagner said, patiently, "Come out of there, you miserable bitch."

On the other side of her bathroom door Lizbeth said nothing.

"We have to leave for the funeral in fifteen minutes, Sis."

In a muffled voice she answered, "I'm not going."

"You are, yes, you are, dear heart."

"I'm sick. I was up half the night with cramps and cold sweats."

"Just another hangover."

"I have the flu. I told you before and you wouldn't listen. And you made me go to that awful service last night."

"Lizbeth."

"You try to order me around like those poor wimps who work for you. I just got worse, going out in that terrible weather."

"Lizbeth." His right hand formed a fist.

"And then that awful man came in and shouted at us."

"Do you know what happened to him?"

After a few seconds she said, "No."

"He was murdered last night," her brother informed her. "Stabbed, just like poor Midge."

"I don't believe you."

"You can read about it on the front page of this morning's *News-Hour.*"

"I don't want to read anything. Please, Kevin, leave me alone."

"Lizbeth." He hit the white wooden door with his big fist. "Come out of there now. Lizbeth! Lizbeth! Lizbeth! Lizbeth! Lizbeth!" Each time he shouted his sister's name he pounded on the door. "Lizbeth! Lizbeth! Lizbeth! Lizbeth!"

"Go away, go away. I'm ill. Please."

"You're going to the funeral, you bitch!" He grabbed the silver doorknob, rattled it violently. "Lizbeth!"

"You're crazy. You're crazy, Kevin. Go away."

"No!" He began kicking at the door. "Lizbeth! Lizbeth! Lizbeth!"

The heavy kicks splintered the wood, but the door held.

"Please, Kevin . . . I'm really very sick. . . ."

"I won't go without you, Sis. If I have to break down the goddamn door . . ." He beat on it with both fists. "Come out! Come out! Come out!"

She didn't say anything.

Wagner took a step back from her bathroom door. His big body was shivering, saliva showed at the edges of his mouth, and his breath rattled in his broad chest.

Very softly he said, "I won't forget this, Sis. Not ever." He left her room.

Matt Prize woke up.

Then he wished he hadn't.

His jaw ached and his abdomen was sore.

"Souvenirs of the late Mr. Garcia." He got out of bed. "Some legacy he left me."

Jan wasn't in bed, but he heard the typewriter rattling away in the den.

Matt's head hurt, too, and his tongue felt muddy and about two or three sizes too big for his mouth.

He opened the drawer of his bureau, the one where he kept half a pound of rocky road fudge for emergencies. The candy was gone.

Getting on a pair of faded jeans and an ancient sweat shirt, Matt made his way to the den. "What's the name of that old movie where Bette Davis won't give her husband his heart medicine?"

"Do I win something if I guess right?" She was sitting at the typewriter, slim shoulders slightly hunched.

"I was making a comparison between that man's act and the hiding of a man's fudge on a morning when . . . ooops!" He entered the room, taking a closer look at her. "You're wearing your hair in braids. That's almost always a bad sign. That demure Heidi look means—"

"Means not a thing. I'm in a working mood is all," she told him. "Max Reinman is reopening the salon tomorrow. I want to hand over a first draft of his brochure right after my class."

Propping himself up against the wall, Matt asked, "Has he hired a replacement for Midge Branner yet?"

"No, Rod's doubling up."

"Let me know who shows up for the class."

She lifted her fingers from the typewriter keys. "You sure you don't want to go to the funeral today?"

"Nope, I have to teach my classes. And then I want to make some notes on this whole business."

"It's all part of the same business, isn't it?"

"Yes. Garcia's murder, Midge's."

Jan said, "The killer is a violent person."

"Agreed."

"And the killer warned you to drop out of the investigation," Jan said. "I know you won't, but . . . well, be extra careful, huh?"

Matt walked over and kissed her. "I'll survive," he promised.

Chapter 18

"WHAT ELSE COULD IT BE?" MAX REINMAN asked morosely. "A jinx, that's what."

The car he and Rod Flanders were riding in made up part of the slow procession that was rolling through the gray, rainy morning from the church to the burial ground in the hills above San Amaro. There were at least forty cars in the cortege.

Flanders, who was driving, said, "You're overreacting, Maxie."

"Sure, sure. My best instructor, present company excepted, gets killed right smack in the middle of my salon," the owner lamented. "That don't exactly provide the sort of publicity which causes customers to come flocking. Then, before Midge is even properly buried, Ernie Garcia gets himself murdered."

"That didn't take place at the Diana Aero—"

"No, but everybody knows Ernie was hanging

around there. And on top of that, he showed up at the funeral parlor last night drunk and mouthing off."

"A coincidence probably."

"A jinx, a curse on me and mine." Reinman slumped further in the passenger seat and watched the rain hit on the windshield. "When I first decided to switch to a dance salon, my sister-in-law Rena—she's the fat one I don't know if you've met her—she told me she had a dream the whole damn place burned down."

"We haven't had any fires."

"Even so, that was an omen."

They'd reached the cemetery road and the parade of cars was winding through woodlands.

"You knew Ernie pretty well," said Flanders.

"Before, years ago. Not since he come out."

"Did you understand what he was talking about last night?"

Reinman didn't respond immediately. "You know what really ticks me off? That son of a bitch Wagner," he said. "Takes over the whole damn funeral, after I'd already offered to pay for it. Takes it over, that's bad enough. But then he don't even ask neither you or me to be pallbearers."

"Just as well, Maxie. It's a terribly stormy day and I, for one, wouldn't relish struggling with her casket over—"

"That ain't the point. The point," explained Reinman, "is you got to pay respect to the dead. The gesture is what counts, even if you get mud on your fancy shoes."

Flanders said, "I was as fond of Midge as you were. And I'm sure she knows it. I don't have to stage a public lamentation, or throw myself in her grave to

145

convey how I feel. It's just something between Midge and myself."

"Who's that smug, fat bastard pick for pallbearers anyway? Six schleps from his own electronics company, people who probably never even knew her."

"Max, she's dead and gone. It doesn't matter."

"Yeah, it matters."

Uphill you could see the gray hearse just passing through the iron gates of the Holy Rest Cemetery. There were a lot of expensive cars in the procession. Beyond the high stone walls you could see acres of tombstones and stone crosses stretching away into the mist.

"The marble orchard," murmured Flanders.

"I wonder if she . . . aw, forget it."

Flanders said, "I was asking you about Ernie Garcia. Last night he was alluding to the robberies he'd been involved in, wasn't he?"

"What do you mean?"

"When he bragged that he had found something, that he had it now. He must've meant some of the missing loot."

"Ernie was punchy."

"No, he knew what he was talking about," said the instructor. "He'd been mixed up with organized crime and somehow Midge walked into it and that's why—"

"Listen," said Max, sitting up, his voice a rasping whisper, "I know Ernie wasn't tied in with the mob. And they had nothing to do with killing him or Midge."

Flanders parked the car at the side of a road. "Who then?"

"Those guys Ernie was working with, they weren't the syndicate," Reinman told him. "They were amateurs, civilians who thought they had a way to make some fast money."

"Who were they?"

"I don't know, he never told me," said Reinman. "Believe me, if I knew I'd fix the bastard who killed Midge. Ernie was maybe asking for it, but not the kid."

"She couldn't have been mixed up with Garcia?"

"Hell, no. Not in any way."

"I didn't think so." Flanders opened the door, stepped out into the morning rain.

Max Reinman lingered. After most of the mourners had left the graveside, after Rod Flanders had gone hurrying downhill to the car.

"I'll be along in a couple minutes," Reinman had told him.

He moved now to the side of Midge's grave. The rain was beating down on the wreaths, knocking over some of the spindly-legged wooden stands, tearing away the white and crimson blossoms.

The rain hit into the grave, too. Drumming on the bronze lid of the casket, turning soggy the six pairs of gray gloves the pallbearers had solemnly thrown into the open grave.

"What a lousy thing to happen," said Reinman, shoulders hunched and hands thrust deep into the pockets of his overcoat. "I'm sorry, kid. Maybe it was my fault. I'm sorry."

Turning away, he began making his way among the gravestones toward the road. People were leaving the cemetery, you could hear car motors grinding to life all up and down the gently sloping hillside.

As Reinman passed a weeping willow tree, someone called out to him. "Don't take it so hard, Mr. Reinman."

He halted, eyes narrowing. "What the hell are you doing here?"

"Can't I pay my respects?" asked Jack Kendig. He wore dark jeans and a down jacket. The hard rain had pushed his hair in scrawls down across his pale forehead. "She was a foxy lady and—"

"Shut up, you scum. Get out of—"

"Easy, Mr. Reinman," advised the youth. "Calling names only causes hard feelings, you know. Yeah, and you're too old to want any trouble."

"The cops are looking for you."

"That's not news."

Angry, Reinman pointed back toward the open grave. "What do you know about that? Did you and those—"

"I didn't cut her up, Mr. Reinman." Kendig smiled thinly. "But I'm not promising, you know, that some of the other ladies who hang around your gym won't get hurt if you don't make a deal with us."

"I make no deals with you, Kendig. And if you keep hassling me, I'm going to put some real tough people on your case," warned Reinman.

"Hey, that really makes me feel uneasy." Chuckling, Kendig eased nearer to the older man. "Now you listen to me, Mr. Reinman, you better start paying your dues before—"

"Maxie? Where are you?"

Flanders was coming up the road on foot, looking for Reinman.

"I'll see you soon again, you know." Kendig pushed by him, went zigzagging away uphill. He dodged tombstones, stepped on old graves, and then the rainy mist swallowed him up.

"Was that Jack Kendig?" asked Flanders when he'd reached his boss's side.

"Yeah, yeah, it was him," answered Reinman. "Let's go home."

"What'd he want?"

"Trouble."

From the lone window in Matt Prize's office on the second floor of Kramer Hall you could see the bell tower that rose up above Faculty Glade. The time was six minutes shy of three. Matt had looked out at the mist-shrouded tower clock several times during the past twenty-five minutes.

A pretty red-haired student, not quite twenty, was sitting across the desk from him. Her smile remained hopeful. "But, Professor Prize, I don't *deserve* a C— on this test," she said, not for the first time.

"I've grasped your position by now, Miss Renfrew. But what you don't seem to—"

"You can call me Pepper."

"Nope, I think not."

She made an exasperated noise, wound her fingers through her long auburn hair. "It's my real name. They christened me that. Pepper Marie Renfrew."

"Catchy." Matt picked up her blue-covered test booklet, closed it, and attempted to return it to her. "The point I want to make, Miss Renfrew, is I can't change the grade."

"But I answered all the questions brilliantly," she persisted. "Take 3A. The description of standard autopsy procedures is very well done, isn't it?"

"Lovingly done. But you can't spell."

149

"Oh, you keep bringing that up, Professor Prize, but we're talking crime fighting here and not literature or something."

He tapped the booklet. "You spell 'villain' *v-i-l-l-i-a-n*."

"Everybody does."

"You spell the possessive 'your' *y-o-u*-apostrophe-*r-e*. But the contraction of 'you' and 'are' you spell *y-o-u-r*."

"That's all minor," complained Pepper Renfrew.

"Not if you want a *B*."

Resting an elbow on the edge of his desk, she gave him an appraising look. "Maybe there's something else I might do to earn a better grade," she suggested, voice low, smiling.

Matt laughed, jumped to his feet, and double-timed to the office door. "Begone, Miss Renfrew," he told her, opening wide the door. "Leave while you have nothing worse than a *C−*, my child."

She remained in her chair. "You're a *young* professor," she said. "And you used to be a private eye. I should think, really, you'd be open to a physical—"

"Shoo, scoot," he instructed her. "And if you try to work your wiles on me again, Miss Renfrew, I'll have you transferred to Professor Dana's section."

She stood, marched out in silence.

Lieutenant Redding nearly bumped into her as he came striding along the corridor. "Excuse me, miss." He stepped aside and then entered Matt's office. "Star pupil?"

"If only she could spell."

Redding dropped into the chair the redhead had been warming for the past half hour. "I don't know how you resist the temptations around here."

"I'm too old for that kind of folly," Matt said, sitting again. "Especially with a young woman who spells until with two *l*'s."

The policeman said, "Nothing much happened at the funeral."

"As is true at most funerals."

"Although Jack Kendig paid a visit." He fished out his pack of cigarettes, placed them on the spot recently occupied by Pepper Renfrew's test booklet.

"You talk to him?"

After lighting his cigarette, the lieutenant shook his head. "He vanished before we even knew he was around," he replied. "He popped out of the bushes, made a try at leaning on Max Reinman, and then took his leave. Flanders told us about the encounter."

Matt tapped at his blotter with a stub of pencil. "Where does Kendig fit in?" he said, mostly to himself.

"Seems to me he fits in about as well as any one at this point."

"Maybe, but . . ." Matt shrugged. "Can I buy you a cup of coffee at the campus canteen? I'm about ready to close up shop."

"Sure, I've got time for that. And we can compare notes."

Matt shook his head. "Not ready for that yet."

Chapter 19

"MAYBE I DON'T NEED A BROCHURE ANY-more." Max Reinman shifted his dead cigar from one side of his mouth to the other. "Instead I should—"

"Nonsense," Jan told him. "This is exactly the time you need a clever advertising campaign." She pushed her twelve pages of typed copy across his desk top and closer to him.

"Look how many ladies didn't show up today. They're afraid to—"

"Only three were missing from our class," she said. "Connie Sloane has dropped out and Mrs. Meyers, but—"

"That guy Sloane. First he's gung ho for his missus to join, then he's practically calling me a crook and demanding a full refund," said Reinman, glancing down at Jan's brochure copy, but not yet picking it up.

"Can't blame him I guess. Poor Midge was murdered right out—"

"Most of us came back. And Lizbeth Wagner ought to return, too, soon as she's over the flu she—"

"Her brother I can do without," confided the salon owner. "The way he took over the funeral. I should of been a pallbearer, but—"

"You should've," agreed Jan. "But that's just not the way Kevin Wagner is. He's used to having his own way."

"He never treated her decent when she was alive, but once poor Midge was dead . . ."

"Lots of people are like that."

Sighing around his unlit stogie, Reinman picked up the copy and started leafing through it. ". . . Convenient location . . . qualified instructors . . . healthful and fun . . . Don't sound bad so far," he remarked. "Select the class best suited to individual needs . . . exercise in safety . . . security guard on duty at all— What?" He took the cigar from between his lips. "Since when do I have a security guard?"

Jan met his gaze. "Mr. Reinman, you're going to have to do something like that," she told him. "For a while at any rate. Fact is, you should've already—"

"Do you know what guards cost? You have any idea what those guys want an hour?"

"Can't be helped." She smiled carefully. "In the long run, it's a heck of a lot cheaper than going bankrupt."

"New locks. First thing Monday I got a guy, he's my second cousin and still he's overcharging me," explained the salon owner. "He's coming over to install new locks on all the doors. And, if we can agree on a price, also a simple burglar alarm system. The place'll be a fort from now—"

"That's all fine, Mr. Reinman, but not enough." She rested her palm on her knee. "We can't mention the murder directly in the brochure, yet we—"

"You bet we can't."

"But everyone who reads our brochure or our new newspaper ads is going to know that there was—"

"What new newspaper ads?"

"You're going to have to do more advertising, Mr. Reinman. To convince people the Diana Aerobic Dance Salon is a perfectly safe place to come to."

"You're going to write the ads for me, too, at highway robbery prices?"

"C'mon." Jan gave a sedate snort. "I'm cheaper than most of the ad agencies in this part of Southern California, and a better writer. You already know that."

He set the copy down. "I got to admit, although it's going to cost me a bundle, that you're right on most counts," acknowledged Reinman. "So what we got to do next is work out a budget. How much for you to write the additional ads, how much to get them ready to run in the *News-Hour,* how much it's going to cost per insertion and so on."

"I can help you do that right now," she offered, reaching into her canvas shoulder bag. "I even brought my pocket calculator along."

The day had died before Jan left the salon.

"Another thing we're going to have to add," she said to herself as she descended to the street, "is more lights on these darned stairs."

She was still two steps from the sidewalk when a shadow loomed up to block her path.

"Please don't scream or make any noise, Miss Early," the young man requested politely. "Can you see what I have in my hand? It's a knife."

Jan fought to keep control of herself. Her heart had started pounding wildly the instant he'd leaped in front of her out of the surrounding darkness. Its beating seemed to be rattling her entire body. "Apparently you know me," she said, realizing her voice no longer sounded quite natural, "but I'm not sure who you—"

"We've been trying to negotiate with Mr. Reinman, you know, but he's a stubborn old bastard."

"Jack Kendig," she said.

Kendig chuckled. "What you're going to do now, Miss Early, is come with us."

"I only write copy for him. I don't have any control over—"

"That's true, but you're a valuable lady," explained Kendig. "You're, you know, worth something to people. Like that college professor you're shacked up with."

"You really don't think you can kidnap me off—"

"Let me explain what you have to do next. It's easy really. You just walk across the sidewalk and climb into the backseat of the blue Mustang that's double-parked there. C'mon, get started."

"Suppose I—"

"No more fooling around." He touched the blade of his knife to her rib cage. "Any noise, any tricky crap, and you end up like Midge Branner."

She inhaled sharply. "You didn't kill Midge."

Kendig laughed. "Move and keep quiet."

Feeling very chill, Jan moved and kept quiet.

Chapter 20

HE ROAMED THE DARK BEACH COTTAGE turning on lights, calling her name.

"Jan? You here?"

Matt checked out the den, then their bedroom. He found no trace of her.

There was no note tacked to the refrigerator, no message taped to the bathroom mirror. The surf was especially loud tonight.

"That meeting with Max Reinman must've dragged on later than she figured."

Returning to the bedroom, Matt changed out of his slightly tweedy professor outfit and into jeans and a T-shirt. The T-shirt, a rarity among those that Jan had given him, had no slogan stenciled front or back.

He straightened up, listening. He'd thought he heard her sports car come driving in. But he'd been wrong.

The night was clear and windy. Dead leaves crackled and whispered as the dark wind worried them across the lawn and over the driveway.

From the den he took a yellow legal tablet and three pens. With those Matt set himself up at the kitchen table. The wall clock showed 7:06.

Opening the tablet, he wrote *Midge Branner/Ernie Garcia* across the top of the first page. On the next line *People.*

"She ought to be home by this time," he said aloud, getting up. Behind a flour sack in the tiny pantry he'd hidden a pair of Mars bars. Jan hadn't discovered them, and he took one, unwrapped it. After carefully crumpling the wrapper into a tight ball, Matt stuffed it far down in the garbage pail. He took the candy bar back to the table.

Max Reinman he wrote.

Rod Flanders.

Kevin Wagner.

Rick Grossman.

Curt Sloane.

Matt set his pen down. "Almost seven-fifteen. Damn, she should be here."

Tad McCrea.

Stew Lofton.

Jack Kendig.

"Wouldn't hurt to phone the salon." He left the table again.

Jan had scribbled the salon number on the list of emergency numbers stuck up next to the wall phone.

"Is that a seven or a four at the end?" Deciding it was a four, Matt dialed.

The phone started to ring. Five times, ten times. No answer. Matt hung up.

To be on the safe side he tried again, substituting a seven for a four.

On the third ring the phone was answered. "Slepyan's Pharmacy. May we serve you?"

"Wrong number, sorry."

Seated once more at the table, he wrote *Diamonds* on a line of its own. Below that went *Who had?* and *Where hid?*

Nearly 7:25.

Returning to the phone, he dialed Norm Levine.

"I mailed you that check a week ago," answered the reporter on the third ring.

"Strangely enough, this isn't one of your creditors."

"Matthew, what's happening, old chum? Have you solved the case?"

"Not quite."

"You sound unhappy. Would you like to pretend this is Dial-A-Joke and have me tell you the one about—"

"You probably haven't, but did you happen to see Jan around town this afternoon?"

Norm answered, "No, I don't think so. Was I supposed to? Am I perhaps having an affair with her that my senile brain keeps forgetting to alert me to?"

"She had a class at Reinman's salon; then she was going to talk over a copywriting job with him. I expected her home quite awhile ago. That's all."

"The salon's open for business as usual again? I ought to do a few pithy paragraphs about that," he said. "Are you worried that the fair Jan is having a furtive candlelit dinner in some swank bistro with our local Terpsichore tycoon?"

"My worry is nonspecific thus far," explained Matt. "Hell, I guess I'm antsing over nothing, Norm."

"Every now and then I get to worrying that my latest wife's run off. So far, though, no such luck," said Norm. "Just kidding, my pet . . . she's lurking nearby . . . Hon, don't throw *that*."

"I'll leave you to your domestic bliss."

"Call me when she finally turns up," said the reporter. "And do let me know soon as you solve these murders. You promised me an exclusive."

"Talk to you later."

As soon as Matt hung up, the phone rang.

"Hello?"

"You're a tough man to reach, Mr. Prize. Your line's always busy. How are you tonight?"

Matt couldn't place the thin, youthful voice. "I don't think I'm certain whom I'm talking to."

"Doesn't matter. The important thing, you know, is you have to get ten-thousand dollars ready damn soon."

"What the hell are you—"

"You keep interrupting, hey, you're sure going to miss something. Listen careful, Mr. Prize. You got twenty-four hours to raise the money. We'll get back to you, you know, as to where we make the exchange."

"What am I buying with this money?"

A dry chuckle. "Shit, glad you reminded me. We got Jan Early, Mr. Prize. The ten-thousand dollars is to get her back. And I got to tell you, I'd hate to have to hurt her. She's pretty, if you like them skinny. I'll be honest with you, you know, I'm having some touble keeping my friends from screwing the lady right now. But I told them we can't fool around with her for at least twenty-four hours. After that—"

"Let me talk to her."

159

"No. You'll just have to take my word."

"I have to know you have her and that she's alive. Otherwise, no deal."

"She's alive."

"Put her on."

There was a silence. "Okay, hold on."

Matt looked at the clock: 7:49.

"She's going to talk to you now. Not long, no funny shit."

"Jan?"

"Hi, Matt."

"You okay?"

"Feeling sort of low," she answered carefully. "Which is funny, since I would've been in my element here at—"

"You've talked enough. Get the ten-thousand dollars, Mr. Prize, and don't talk to the cops." The phone went dead.

Lieutenant Redding lit a cigarette. "It's got to be Jack Kendig who's got her."

"Afraid so," said Matt. "What's he likely to do to her?"

"You can't tell with him. Kendig isn't exactly stable. He explodes every now and then and does something crazy."

Matt walked over to the large map of Norfield on the wall of the lieutenant's office. "Jan was trying to pass me information on where she is."

"People are always reading meanings into—"

"Nope, I'm not imagining this." Matt reached out, tapped the map. "She said she was feeling low."

"Who wouldn't be?"

Matt said, "That's got to be part of the location,

damn it. Low. A cellar, a basement. Some place underground."

"If we knew which cellar Kendig and his gang were holed up in at the moment, we'd have brought him in already."

"She also told me she would've been in her element."

"Meaning?"

"That was, I'm pretty sure, a reference to the fact she's a vegetarian."

Redding told him, "You're reaching for it, Matt."

"Along Marcus Street here," he said as he traced the street with his finger, "there are several abandoned stores and warehouses. Now these three buildings right here were, as recently as three or four years ago, produce warehouses."

"That much is true."

"What do they keep in produce warehouses? Vegetables."

Lieutenant Redding blew out a swirl of smoke. "Jan could just as easily be in the cellar of a vegetarian restaurant or—"

"She told me she *would've*, meaning the place wasn't what it used to be anymore," Matt insisted. "Besides, there are only two vegetarian restaurants in San Amaro. Stew Lofton's and that lesbian joint out on the highway. It's unlikely Kendig is in cahoots with either."

"You want me to go with you and poke into those rundown old warehouses on Marcus?"

"I do, yeah."

The lieutenant said, "We'll do that, Matt. And if she isn't there, then I'm afraid it's going to be the usual slow and patient police routine."

Chapter 21

THE THICKSET BLOND YOUNG MAN WITH THE coiled snake tattooed on the back of his right hand said, "I'm Rudy."

Jan said nothing.

"Why don't you say, 'Hi, Rudy. Nice to meet you'?"

"Guess I'm not in the mood."

She was sitting on the cold stone floor of the damp basement, hands tied behind her with black electrical tape and ankles similarly wrapped. Piled high around her were old wooden crates. Their faded labels said things like Buddy Boy Carrots, Pride O' Napa Grapes, Farmer Joe Tomatoes.

Rudy was squatting close to her, a hunting knife held in one hand with the glittering blade resting across the palm of his other hand. There were three other young men, including Jack Kendig, lounging around the big, low room. An old table lamp glowed on an upturned crate and there was a raw bulb in the dangling ceiling fixture.

Kendig was sitting in a canvas deck chair, a telephone on the floor near him. "Quit annoying her, Rudy."

"I'm not annoying her. He says I'm annoying you. Am I annoying you?"

She turned her head away.

"Am I annoying you? I said."

"Matter of fact, yes."

Laughing, Rudy touched her cheek with the tip of his knife. "Does this annoy you?"

"I don't think you'd better cut me," Jan said carefully. "Otherwise—"

"Who's cutting you? I'm only making conversation. Isn't that what you like to do? You and your college asshole professor. Sit around and make conversaton. He's a fag, isn't he?"

The tip of the knife traced a lazy S on her face, not quite breaking the skin.

"I hear he's a faggot. Isn't that true?"

Kendig chuckled, but ordered, "Rudy, quit."

Rudy moved the knife until the tip rested against her blouse just above her left breast. "I'm smart myself," he told her. "Sure. I'm the one got the electricity going again in this place and rigged the phone. And the light and power assholes and the phone company don't even know. Could a faggot college professor do that?"

Jan shut her eyes.

"I don't think he could," Rudy answered for himself. "No, I don't think that fag you live with can do anything. I bet he can't even screw you. Can he?"

He drew, very lightly, a circle around her breast with the knife blade.

"You don't like that asshole, do you?" continued Rudy. "If you liked him, hell, you'd argue with me. Maybe there's nothing to argue about. I guess he never screwed you. Nobody ever did maybe."

Kendig warned, "Rudy, get away from her now."

"Would you like me to?" Rudy asked her. "Hey, I'm talking to you."

With his free hand he took hold of her hair, tilted her head back.

She opened her eyes. "Please."

"Please what? You mean, please, Rudy, do it? Or, please, Rudy, get your grungy hands off me? Which do you mean?"

Kendig was on his feet. "I don't want her marked up."

"I'm not marking her up. He says I'm marking you up. Am I marking you up?"

"I'm afraid I can't tell."

"I ain't marking you at all. If I was, you'd know it. You'd be bleeding, it'd hurt."

Kendig came nearer, stood looking down at them. "That's enough," he said. "For now anyway."

Lieutenant Redding drove the unmarked car along the night street. The abandoned buildings loomed on either side, dark and lifeless. The street lamps provided the only illumination. At the intersection of Marcus and Third a gust of wind blew tatters of old newspaper across the path of their headlights.

"You spot him?" the lieutenant asked.

"In the alley between the Macri Brothers produce

warehouse and the Cassiday Paper Bag factory, yeah," answered Matt. "Pretty sure he's a look-out."

"I'd agree." He snuffed out his cigarette in the car ashtray. "Maybe your hunch is right. That guy could be one of Kendig's bunch."

"Why don't you park around the corner," suggested Matt.

"What're you figuring on doing?"

"Having a talk with their lookout."

Nodding, the policeman turned the next corner and eased over to the curb. The car wheels crunched over the remnants of a cardboard packing case. "I'll cruise back up there in ten minutes. That give you enough time?"

"Ought to." Matt left the car.

The night wind whipped at him, rubbed dirt in his eyes.

As he passed a shadowy doorway near the corner, something suddenly stirred.

"Happy birthday!" shouted a rough-edged, throaty voice.

Matt pivoted, faced the doorway.

"Is it your birthday or mine?" asked the pudgy derelict who came tottering forth. "Hell, it doesn't matter. Long as we go buy us another bottle."

"Not just yet."

"What do you mean? What do you mean?" demanded the threadbare drunk loudly. "You mean you're too low-down and rotten to have a drink with a poor lonely old man on his goddamn birthday? Or your birthday? Whosoever's it is." He was no more than forty. His face was puffy, smudged with several days' stubble and splotched with cuts and bruises in several stages of healing. "Is that the sort of lousy no good son of a bitch you're turning out to be?"

Matt took hold of the man's shoulder, fingers gripping the soiled cloth of his tattered sport jacket. "No, I'm the sort of son of a bitch," he told him quietly, "who's going to knock you flat on your ass unless you crawl back into your hole right now and shut up."

The drunk blinked. "I thought you was somebody else, mister," he mumbled. Jerking free, he went stumbling back to his doorway and was quickly lost in shadows.

Matt moved on.

Somewhere, a couple of blocks away, a stray dog started howling. Farther off, an ambulance siren shrilled.

A quarter of a block from the old Macri Brothers building Matt ducked into an alley. He nearly stepped right on a dead cat as he made his way to the metal fire ladder he'd spotted earlier. The pale bluish light of the nearest street lamp gave the rich and varied debris underfoot a dead, underwater tint.

He caught hold of a rusty rung and started upward. The brick building, once a tool factory, was four stories high. In more recent times the tar-papered roof had been used for impromptu social events. There was a greasy single-bed mattress slumped near the ventilator chimney, amidst a scatter of collapsed beer cans and a bedraggled pair of pantyhose draped across the darkness.

Bent low, he hurried across the rooftop. The next building was the former home of the Cassiday bag works and the roof was on the same level and about four feet distant.

Nodding once, not looking down, Matt leaped.

Landing safely, he walked across the roof to its far edge. Below him four stories, leaning casually at the mouth of the alley and smoking a self-made cigarette, was the dark-haired young man they'd noticed earlier.

The metal fire escape stairway that dropped from this roof would bring him down about fifteen yards from the lookout's back.

If Matt could get down the damn thing without giving himself away.

He took a quick deep breath, began his descent.

The wind brushed at him, tugging at his clothes.

He went down slowly and carefully. A step and a pause, a step and a pause.

While he was still halfway from the ground somebody started yelling down on the street.

Matt froze.

"Happy birthday, kid! Happy birthday to you. Or is it me?" It was the drunk. He'd left his hole and come tottering along the street.

"Get away from me, you old fart," warned the youth.

Matt resumed his downward climb.

"One bottle of muskydoodle is all we need," the derelict was patiently explaining. "Oh, and maybe a nice chocolate cake with birthday candles. So let's go get— Ow! Jesus!"

"Now get away."

"Jesus, you broke something. Honest to god." His voice had grown thin and fearful. "You hurt me and— Ow! Don't hit me any—"

"Get out of here, you old scumbag!"

Matt dropped from the last rung to the ground.

Swiftly and silently he moved toward the preoccupied lookout's back.

The young man was getting ready to hit the drunk once more.

Lunging, Matt caught his arm. He jerked it around behind the youth's back and twisted hard.

"Hey, man, what the hell—"

"Quiet," suggested Matt, yanking the arm further up.

"You're hurting my—"

"Just shut up."

The drunk was sitting on the sidewalk now, his dirty and scabby hands clutching his midsection. Tears were wobbling down his face. "I can't breathe anymore," he complained in a puzzled whisper.

Matt told the young man, "Show me where Kendig is."

"Go screw your—"

"Tell me. Right quick." He increased the pressure on the arm.

Gritting his teeth, the lookout made a whimpering noise. "You'll get yourself—"

"Where is he?"

"Under the old produce warehouse there," he answered in a gasp. "You got to use that metal, side door, see. Then go down the back stairs to the basement."

"In a minute, when my associate gets here, you're going to take us there."

"I'm going to take you straight to— Okay, okay, asshole. I'll take you."

"It really isn't," decided the rueful drunk, "anybody's birthday at all."

Jack Kendig rose from his chair, his left hand yanking out the knife from his pocket. "What the hell are you doing down here, Rosco?"

Rosco, the lookout, made a sideways, staggering entrance into the produce warehouse basement. Due chiefly to the propelling shove in the back given him by Matt's hand.

"The goddamn cops," he muttered, stopping against a crate.

"That's right, fellows," said Lieutenant Redding, who'd followed Matt into the underground room. He had a .38 revolver in his hand.

"Shit," observed Kendig. He dropped his knife to the floor.

"Evening, Jack," said the lieutenant as he moved farther inside the room. "Chuck, Skip, Rudy."

Matt was crossing to where Jan sat. "You okay?"

"More or less."

Kendig asked, "How the hell'd you know we were here?"

The policeman answered, "Police procedures."

"You better not try to take me," warned Rudy, who was close to the bound young woman. His hunting knife was in his hand. "I'll slice her up, man, and you, too."

Matt stopped, watching him. "No, you won't."

"Like hell. Just— Hey!"

Matt had dived at him suddenly. He tackled him, tipped him over, and at the same time grabbed his knife hand.

The knife flew free of Rudy's fingers, clattered on the stone floor.

Matt came to his feet, straddling him.

He grabbed him by the shirtfront, hit him twice across the face with his other hand.

Then he let go of him, picked up the knife, and started cutting at the tape that held Jan.

"Come on over here and line up, Rudy," said Redding. "No more kidding around, huh?"

"Assholes," said Rudy. But he got to his feet and went to stand where he was told.

"I'm glad," said Jan quietly, "you found me."

Matt said, "I'm sort of pleased myself."

Chapter 22

MATT CLOSED THE BEACH COTTAGE DOOR against the last of the departing news people. "Some of those folks made Norm Levine look shy."

"I specially liked the one who wanted to videotape a few minutes of my getting ready for bed."

"That might make an interesting news segment."

Jan was on the sofa, legs up and an extra pillow behind her head. "Actually Norm himself was very sweet and thoughtful. Asked his questions and left."

"Yes, he's a good lad. We'll have to nominate him for a Pulitzer." Matt leaned against the arm of the sofa, looking down at her.

"Alone at last," said Jan. "What time is it anyway? Never mind, I'd rather not know."

"We've definitely entered what is known technically as the wee hours."

"Oh, did I tell you I'm going to get an extra fifteen-hundred dollars out of Max Reinman."

"You didn't. Congratulations."

Slowly, her fatigue showing, Jan sat up. "I know I've been behaving bravely, like Wonder Woman or some equally tough broad," she said. "But . . . oh, Matt, I was scared as hell the whole damned time."

Sitting beside her, he put an arm around her shoulders. "Everybody gets scared. But you handled yourself just fine."

"Better I handled myself than Kendig and his gang." She rested her cheek against his chest. "I'm not certain how far they would've gone, Matt, but I think it's a good thing you got there when you did."

"They didn't get a chance to hurt you?"

"Only verbally." She shuddered. "Did you notice that snake tattoo on Rudy's hand? When he talked about what he might do to me . . . It was such an unsettling mixture of lust and cold detachment."

"You really want to talk about this now?"

"What you mean is I don't have to."

"I don't need an instant replay, but I want to hear whatever you want to talk about."

Jan said, "Knives. They all had knives. Nobody cut me, only almost. Trouble was I got to where I couldn't tell how far they'd go."

"It's all over."

"There are a lot of fairly rotten people in the world."

"I've noticed."

"I really don't see how somebody like Lieutenant Redding can keep it up."

"He smokes a lot." Matt stroked her blond hair.

"Excuse my babbling."

"You're entitled."

"Do you think Jack Kendig killed Midge?"

"His name's on my list."

"But it isn't the only name, huh?"

"Nope."

She said, "This has been what you might call an eventful and stressful day. The wise thing to do would be to take a couple of tranquilizers and pass into oblivion as fast as possible. However . . . Would you think I was especially silly if I suggested we make love instead?"

"Not at all," he assured her.

The morning was clear, warm and bright. Matt awakened early, just as the sunlight was touching their bedroom windows.

He sat up in bed, watching the sleeping Jan.

She was on her side, knees tucked up, one hand near her chin. Although her pretty face was relaxed, the fingers of her hand were tightly clenched.

Matt touched her blond hair and she murmured softly but didn't waken.

Carefully he got out of bed. After quickly dressing, Matt journeyed to the kitchen.

While he was fixing himself a bowl of Rice Krispies, using chocolate milk to inspire them to snap, crackle, and pop, the phone sounded.

"Hello?"

"All well with you?" inquired Norm.

"We're fine."

"Jan's getting along well?"

"Yep."

The reporter said, "Knowing me, old chum, you are aware I'm usually a crass and callous fellow. Nonetheless, I don't want to bother you this early in the A.M. . . . but, hell, I was worried. You both looked a mite bedraggled last night."

"Since we are friends," said Matt, grinning, "I won't ever mention to anyone that you're an old softie who cares about his friends."

Norm asked, "You need anything?"

"Nothing."

"Long as I've got you . . . what about the murder case? The cops are holding Jack Kendig and crew, but Redding'll only discuss the abduction charges," said the reporter. "Does that mean Kendig didn't kill either Midge Branner or Ernie Garcia?"

"I think I've just about got this mess figured out," Matt told him. "I'm planning to go over my notes this morning."

"And then?"

"Been toying with the notion of getting all the interested parties together. At the salon. For a discussion of my conclusions."

"Will Redding go along with that?"

"He should."

"Do I get an invite?"

"Your name heads the list."

"Keep in touch then, *amigo*. My best to Jan."

Before he settled down with his bowl of cereal, Matt fetched his legal tablet from the den. He opened it to the page with the list of names he'd made last night.

As he ate, he ran the blank end of his pen along the list. He ate slowly, pausing quite a lot to stare up at the ceiling and at the new day out beyond the kitchen windows.

By the time he was swallowing the last spoonful, he'd crossed off three names.

Matt pushed the empty bowl aside, rested both elbows on the table. "Nope, he won't fit either," he said, drawing a quick line through yet another name.

Ten minutes later he straightened up, nodding his head and smiling to himself. "Of course," he said aloud, crossing out all the names but one. "There's only one possible person who can be the killer."

Home delivery from Pocket Books

Here's your opportunity to have fabulous bestsellers delivered right to you. Our free catalog is filled to the brim with the newest titles plus the finest in mysteries, science fiction, westerns, cookbooks, romances, biographies, health, psychology, humor—every subject under the sun. Order this today and a world of pleasure will arrive at your door.

POCKET BOOKS, Department ORD
1230 Avenue of the Americas, New York, N.Y. 10020

Please send me a free Pocket Books catalog for home delivery

NAME _____

ADDRESS _____

CITY _____ STATE/ZIP _____

If you have friends who would like to order books at home, we'll send them a catalog too—

NAME _____

ADDRESS _____

CITY _____ STATE/ZIP _____

NAME _____

ADDRESS _____

CITY _____ STATE/ZIP _____